"You okay?"

A deep clearing of his throat brought her attention back to the guy outside the car. He tilted his head with the question.

Destiny noticed he'd leaned against the pump and crossed his arms, which drew more attention to biceps that would put every guy in her Atlanta gym to shame. And she suspected from his letters that he wasn't the kind of guy to hit a gym. He'd mentioned putting in a good, honest day's work every day. She also knew that he'd support his wife's choice if she wanted to work outside the home, but if she decided to be a stay-at-home mom, he'd support that just as much.

She knew so much about this guy, but he didn't know the first thing about her. She'd have to change that, and she couldn't waste time about it. Those letters could save her magazine. So she had to gain his trust and then get the rights to run them.

No sweat.

Books by Renee Andrews

Love Inspired

Her Valentine Family
Healing Autumn's Heart
Picture Perfect Family
Love Reunited
Heart of a Rancher
Bride Wanted

RENEE ANDREWS

spends a lot of time in the gym. No, she isn't working out. Her husband, a former all-American gymnast, co-owns ACE Cheer Company, an all-star cheerleading company. She is thankful the talented kids at the gym don't have a problem when she brings her laptop and writes while they sweat. When she isn't writing, she's typically traveling with her husband, bragging about their two sons or spoiling their bulldog.

Renee is a kidney donor and actively supports organ donation. She welcomes prayer requests and loves to hear from readers. Write to her at Renee@ReneeAndrews.com, visit her website at www.reneeandrews.com or check her out on Facebook or Twitter.

Bride Wanted
Renee Andrews

HARLEQUIN® LOVE INSPIRED®

Recycling programs for this product may not exist in your area.

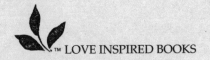 LOVE INSPIRED BOOKS

ISBN-13: 978-0-373-87833-8

BRIDE WANTED

www.LoveInspiredBooks.com

Printed in U.S.A.

Though one may be overpowered,
two can defend themselves.
A cord of three strands is not quickly broken.
—*Ecclesiastes* 4:12

This novel is dedicated to the real Jolaine Bowers, my mom. Mama, I hope you like your character (and before you ask, she's only named after you; it isn't actually you…or that's my story).
I love you, Mom!

Chapter One

"RuthEllen was talking today at her shop about the reason she believes you haven't married, and I think she may have it figured right." Jolaine Bowers peeked beneath the hood of her Camry so that Troy Lee had no choice but to look up and face his grandmother head-on. "Do you want to know what she said?" Her brows were raised and her eyes were so wide he could see white all the way around the blue.

"RuthEllen Riley? At the beauty shop?" Troy wondered how many Claremont ladies had been getting cut, permed or shampooed while RuthEllen chatted about his marital status. Then again, she probably wasn't the only one discussing it if his grandmother had been there, too. "Y'all were talking about me? At the beauty shop? Just how many women were there?"

"The regulars. Maybe a few extra since everyone is getting their hair done before all of the Fourth of July activities this week." His grandmother raised a shoulder. "And we always talk about you, dear. We talk about everyone we care about."

He kept checking the engine on the car. "There's something not quite right about that."

Her mouth flattened. "We only talk about you because we're worried. So, don't you want to know what RuthEllen said?"

He momentarily stopped trying to determine why her car was making what she described as a "weird rattle-rumble kind of sound," climbed out from under the hood and answered her with the only response she'd accept. "Sure, what did she say?"

She stepped away from the car, took a quick breath then spouted, "She said you're a player."

Not at all what Troy expected. "A player?"

His grandmother nodded, then converted the move into one of those subtle head shakes that said she couldn't believe his sad state. "Yes, that's what she said, and everyone in the shop agreed."

It was all Troy could do not to laugh, but she looked so serious that he held it in check. "Does RuthEllen even know what a player is? And do you?"

She fished a bottle of water out of her purse, unscrewed the lid and took a long swallow. Then she twisted the top on and dropped it back in. "I'll be honest. I didn't know until the girls at the shop explained it, but from what they say, it's a guy who, you know, acts like he is interested in a girl and then drops her like a hot potato." She settled her purse strap on her shoulder. "That's you."

He grabbed a shop rag from his back pocket, wiped the sweat from his brow and tried to determine the best way to explain to his sweet grandmother the difference between being a player and being selective.

"I'm not a player. I just don't continue dating someone if I can't see myself marrying her."

"That's what I told RuthEllen, but she said that's called leading them on, and I'm thinking she might be right. Troy, you've dated nearly every girl in Claremont once. Sometimes twice, but mostly once. They get their hopes up, and then you're gone."

Troy winced at the truth of her statement. He'd realized the same thing recently, when it seemed every time he ran into a female in town he received the awkward "what went wrong?" stare.

She grabbed her water bottle again and tilted it toward his face. "See, you know it's true. But I don't think it's that you're *trying* to be a player. You've set the bar too high, with all of that letter writing you do and envisioning the woman you want to marry and all. That was supposed to get you started thinking about the kind of woman you want. It wasn't supposed to exclude every girl from fitting the bill."

"I'm beginning to think I shouldn't have even told you about those letters." Troy had assumed his grandmother would instinctively understand the importance of those letters to his future bride. Now he wondered if every lady at the Cut and Curl knew about them. "You didn't tell RuthEllen and the other ladies about them, did you?"

She blinked, twice. "No…why?"

"Because they're private. I wrote them to one person, and she's the only one I plan to share them with." He paused. "Assuming I ever find her." Troy's first letter to his future bride had been written when he was twelve as an assignment at church camp. Most kids wrote the required letter and then let that be it, but he'd continued over the years. And as he wrote to her, he'd clearly defined the woman he wanted to spend his life with.

He just hadn't found her yet.

"Well." She chewed on her lower lip. "I didn't tell the girls at the shop about your letters, dear." She looked as though she wanted to say more, maybe ask if he'd reconsider letting her share the fact that he'd been writing for over a decade and a half to a wife he hadn't met, but then she must have thought better of the idea and snapped her mouth shut.

"That's good," he said. "I appreciate you keeping that to yourself."

"You're probably right." She fidgeted with the water bottle again. "I shouldn't tell anyone about your love letters."

"I'd appreciate that."

"Right," she whispered.

Troy had returned his attention to the engine but heard a hint of worry in her tone, so he looked back to his sweet grandmother, twisting the lid on and off the bottle. "Hey, it's okay that y'all were talking about me at the shop. I understand that's what ladies do, and I understand you do it because you care about me. I'd just rather the love-letter part stay out of any conversations, okay?"

She nodded and gave him a little smile. "Okay. Well, RuthEllen and the other ladies and I all decided what you need to do. You need to find someone who didn't grow up in Claremont, someone who doesn't know you're a player."

"I'm *not* a player." Troy couldn't hold back his grin now, finding a lot of humor in making the statement to his grandmother. And while he was supposed to be working, no less. Luckily Bo and Maura Taylor trusted him to get all of his work done at their filling station, and they also understood his grandmother's need to visit him at his job place every now and again.

"Troy Alan Lee, this is not funny. You're twenty-seven years old."

His grin grew. He couldn't help it. "You know, I've heard of guys who didn't get married until they were in their forties."

"Not in Claremont." Her hands weren't fidgeting now, and she uncapped her water bottle to take another swig.

He set his laugh free. "No, probably not in Claremont, but twenty-seven isn't ancient. And just so you know, I have a date with a girl on Friday who I'm sure doesn't see me as a player."

She capped the bottle and tossed it back in her purse. "Really? Who is she?"

Troy could tell from the excitement in her tone that she'd probably make a beeline straight to RuthEllen's shop when she left the filling station with the glorious news. "Don't go getting too anxious. It's a first date, but her name is Haley Calhoun. She moved here from Florida to take a veterinarian job with Doc Sheridan. He's planning to retire in a few years and decided he needed an assistant, someone who could get familiar with all of the families and livestock and such in the area."

A bright smile claimed his grandmother's face.

"That's perfect! She isn't from around here, so she won't know about how you date and run. Maybe she's the one meant to get your letters. You concentrate on making it to at least date number three, and I'll make sure to tell all the girls at the beauty shop and in my quilting group not to say anything to her about you being a player."

He knew better than to try to stop her, so he nodded. "You do that." Then he opened the driver's side door and climbed in. "I didn't see anything under the hood that would cause that rattling you described. Let me drive it and see if I hear the noise, too."

"Sounds good. I'll go inside the store and visit with Maura. I'm so excited about your date with the Calhoun girl. I have a good feeling about this." Grinning, she turned and headed toward the store connected to the garage.

He cranked the car and took it for a short drive away from the station. And while he drove, he thought about the fact that he was evidently now seen as a "player" around town. The absurdity of that was laughable. He wasn't a player, but he had dated a lot of girls, most of them in town, he supposed. And he hadn't gotten serious with any of them. He'd always thought God would make it clear when he met the right one, but maybe all of the letters he'd been writing had clouded his vision. He hadn't given anyone a chance because he had his sights set on perfection. No one was perfect; Troy knew that. But he'd really thought he would know when he met the girl he'd been writing to all these years. He hadn't considered the fact that it might take more than a date or two to determine whether he'd met "the one."

God, help me out here. Part of me thinks my grandmother is right. I haven't given anyone a chance. Help me to see clearly this time, Lord. And help me to know when I meet the right person, and to spend enough time with her to tell. I want to at least see what could happen with Haley. If You could somehow show me whether she's the girl for me, I'd sure appreciate the help. In Jesus's name, amen.

He pulled back into the station and heard the horrid rattle that his grandmother described. He'd heard it a few times throughout the short drive, and it hadn't taken him long to pinpoint the source of the hideous noise. But he couldn't miss the fun of showing her, so he waited for her to come outside to identify the problem. Maura Taylor walked alongside her as she neared the car.

"Well, did you hear it?" Jolaine asked.

"I did. And you're right, it's a horrible racket. I don't know how you've put up with it."

She nodded. "I know. It's been driving me crazy for the past week. How bad is it? Do I need a new car, or is it something you can fix? Tell me it's something you can fix."

"Definitely something I can fix." He climbed out, then squatted down by the driver's seat. "And I can take care of it right now without a single tool." Sliding his hand under the seat, he withdrew an empty water bottle, then another and another. He pulled six bottles out from under the seat, while Maura muffled her laughter with her hand over her mouth.

"Is *that* what was making the racket? Those bottles rolling under the seat? James would get on me big-time. Don't tell your grandfather, Troy. I've been meaning to clean out the car."

"I won't tell him, but I'm not sure you'll get so lucky with Mr. Taylor knowing."

Her cheeks reddened as Bo Taylor neared the group and didn't attempt to stifle his laughter. She pointed a finger at the man. "You keep quiet, Bo."

"I'll make sure he does," Maura promised.

"I think you'll find your ride much more peaceful now." Troy tossed the empty bottles in a nearby can.

"Thank you, Troy." She kissed his cheek. "Anyway, I got to visit with you and let you know about what you need to do."

"Yes, you did." Troy knew she didn't mean any harm, and he loved her dearly for her attempt to help his love life. Maybe she even steered him in the right direction. He had been a bit picky, and thanks to her visit, he'd made a conscious decision to rectify that soon, this Friday, in fact, with Haley Calhoun. One way or another, he'd make it to date number three.

Destiny Porter sat in her car and waited at the end of the line for gas, all the while watching the mechanic in the garage to the right of the filling station. He wore traditional blue coveralls, and she could tell he had thick, jet-black hair, broad shoulders and a lean waist, but that was it.

She'd left her apartment in Atlanta, packed her things for an indefinite stay and then driven 120 miles to Claremont, Alabama, to see the man and convince him to share his love letters with the world. And now he had his head tucked under the hood of a car.

"Come on, turn around." Her plea was interrupted when an older version of Richard Gere tapped on her window. Destiny rolled it down. "Yes?"

"Ma'am, I can't reach your tank unless you pull up to the pump." He glanced over his shoulder to see what held her attention. The mechanic had finally come out from under the hood and had moved to a bevy of tools against the opposite side wall. "Aah, so you're another of Troy's admirers. I wonder if I shouldn't start paying him some sort of commission for all of the extra customers I get." The man chuckled then nodded toward the pump, still several feet away. "Why don't you move forward a little so I can at least pump your gas while you're doing a rather pitiful attempt at flirting long-distance?"

"Oh, I wasn't, or, I didn't mean to stare."

He raised a dark gray brow.

Destiny felt her cheeks flame. "I've never even met the man." And that was the truth. But she did know everything he wanted in a woman and how he'd treat the one who earned his love, which was why she'd made this trip. However, she wouldn't share that with this man. She also wouldn't share it with the mechanic, who apparently had *lots* of admirers around town.

He'd have plenty more if he let her publish those letters.

She decided she'd change the subject and attempt to save herself any further embarrassment while the man removed the nozzle and busied himself with his work.

"I don't think I've ever been to a real full-service gas station."

He nodded as he put gas in her red Beemer. "I suspected as much. You aren't from around here." He pointed a knowing finger toward Destiny's face. "Claremont's a small town. Everyone knows everyone, and I'm pretty sure if you were from around here, I'd have noticed." He glanced toward the garage. "But it isn't my attention you're trying to get anyway, is it? Not that it'd matter. I'm happily taken." He winked. "So, you just passing through or staying awhile?"

Destiny wished she could control her traitorous eyes, but the guy in the garage had finally faced her and she was, quite frankly, speechless.

The older man cleared his throat. "I'm Bo Taylor, by the way. The lady who just walked into the station is my wife, Maura. Assuming you're listening to my rambling and all."

Destiny blushed again. She couldn't remember the last time she was so embarrassed. "I—I'm sorry. I don't mean to…"

"Yeah, you do, but that's okay. Every young lady from town comes here as often as possible." Bo frowned as the nozzle clattered and the gas stopped pumping. "This isn't full yet. Let me get her started back up." He flipped the silver lever on the pump and the thing clicked to life again. "Tell you what, I'll go get Troy and offer an introduction. The customer line is gone now anyway."

"No, that's okay. I don't want to disturb him."

The man nodded once as though the matter was decided, ignored Destiny's protest and started toward the garage. And the gas, which was taking *forever* to pump, clicked to a near standstill when he walked away. Destiny didn't even know the numbers could turn that slowly, but then again, all of the gas stations in Atlanta had digital displays. This one, like everything else she'd seen so far, seemed straight out of the 1950s. And since it continued turning slower than traffic on I-285 at rush hour, she barely had three gallons in the tank when Bo returned with tall, dark and mesmerizing Troy Lee by his side.

He was a good six-two, easy, the jet-black hair even darker shining in the sun. Destiny's hands involuntarily tightened on the wheel, and she made her fingers relax so the blood could start flowing again. Did he really look this good, or was it the fact that she already knew so much about the man and the thoughts of his heart that made her feel as if she were going to pass out merely looking at him? The subscribers to her magazine would simply have to have a photo to accompany his love letters…once Destiny had the authority to put them in print. Which she'd have, one way or another, before next month's issue. She had to; she'd already promised her advertisers.

"Troy, this is…" Bo Taylor waited for her to fill in the blank.

"Destiny," she said. "Destiny Porter."

"Nice to meet you." He gave her an easy smile, and a deep dimple popped in place slightly beneath his left cheekbone. Somehow that single indention made him even more incredible.

"She's from out of town, but I didn't find out yet if

she's passing through or staying awhile." He looked again to Destiny.

She really had to get a grip. "I'm from Atlanta. Staying awhile."

Bo nodded. "Troy, my throat is parched. I thought that line of customers was never going to die down, but Ms. Destiny is the last one for now. Can you finish up here? I'm going to head on in and get a soda with Maura."

"Sure." Troy nodded at the man retreating to the station and didn't seem to notice how guilty he looked as he left Destiny to deal with her unwanted attraction on her own. She did *not* need to be distracted by his looks. She simply needed his signature on a contract, a contract that would allow her to expose his innermost thoughts to the world.

Nervous, she looked away from the handsome country boy and spotted the latest copy of her magazine in the passenger's seat, as well as a printout of the email that caused her to take this trip. And the love letters—this man's love letters. She reached into the backseat, grabbed her gigantic purse and flung it over the evidence.

A deep clearing of his throat brought her attention back to the guy outside the car. "You okay?" He tilted his head with the question.

Destiny noticed he'd leaned against the pump and crossed his arms, which drew more attention to biceps that would put every guy in her Atlanta gym to shame. And she suspected from his letters that he wasn't the kind of guy to hit a gym. He'd mentioned putting in a good, honest day's work every day. She also knew that he'd support his wife's choice if she wanted to work outside the home, but if she decided to be a stay-at-home mom, he'd support that just as much.

She knew so much about this guy, but he didn't know the first thing about her. She'd have to change that, and she couldn't waste time about it. Those letters could save her magazine. So she had to gain his trust and then get the rights to run them.

No sweat.

But she was sweating now, and she didn't think it was necessarily due to the Alabama heat. Did all guys down here look like that?

Destiny saw that he still waited for her to answer his question. "Oh, yes, I'm fine. Just wanted to have my purse handy when it's time to pay." She shot a glance at the churning pump. "I'm guessing the customer lines have something to do with the speed of the pumps?"

He laughed, and the sound rippled over her skin like cocoa butter on a hot day at the beach. She'd have never thought a guy from a tiny town in Alabama could have this effect on her senses. Then again, she'd have never thought a guy from here would be as sensitive and heartfelt as the one standing beside her car.

But he didn't know she knew about that. She snuck a glance at her passenger seat to make sure his letters were covered.

"So, you said you're staying awhile. What are you planning to do in Claremont? We aren't exactly the tourist capital of the world, other than the dude ranch and the fishing camp. But you don't seem like the dude-ranch or fishing-camp type." He shrugged broad shoulders. "No offense."

"None taken." She felt her heart rate slow and was glad she was becoming more at ease talking to the guy who'd so thoroughly, and unknowingly, touched her heart. "I'm staying a few weeks to write stories about life in a small Southern town." That was true; she did plan to write about Claremont and about the couples she'd meet during her visit, as her magazine focused on love, but that wasn't what brought her here.

Troy Lee did.

"Well, then, you've come to the right place. You don't get much smaller than Claremont." He sighed, a nearly inaudible sound, but one Destiny heard, since she hung on to every word. "But in my opinion, we've got everything anyone could need."

And there it was, the sentimental side she'd sensed in his letters and the guy who'd treat a girl like pure gold. Destiny fought the urge to sigh right back. However, she'd dated quite a few guys who started out acting that way and then their true colors came shining through, thicker and darker than hard Georgia clay. She hadn't met an honest, sincere one yet. But if Troy Lee's letters to his future bride rang true, he could be the real deal. And the type her readers wanted to hear about.

She cleared her throat. "So, what does Claremont have, besides the dude ranch and the fishing camp?"

He grinned. "I was right. You aren't the dude-ranch or fishing-camp kind of girl."

She found it very easy to smile at Troy. "I'll be honest. I'm afraid of horses, but truthfully, I've always wanted to learn how to fish."

"Really, now? Well, I might be able to help you out."

Destiny already knew that, of course, but she kept her poker face intact. "How could you do that?"

"It just so happens that I have a second job on the weekends running the fishing hole. It isn't as organized and all as the new fish camp. The Cutter family owns that, and it's more of a vacation spot. But my grandparents James and Jolaine Bowers own the fishing hole, and it's the type of place to go if you want to have some quiet time for a day, relax outside, take in the scenery."

"And catch some fish?"

His dimple popped back into place with his smile. "Yeah, that, too."

"So you'll be there this weekend?" Destiny was doing a little fishing right now, and she wasn't all that discreet about it, but he didn't seem to mind.

"I will." He reached into his back pocket and withdrew a leather wallet. "I think I have a couple of their cards left in here. I'll get you one. It'll have the address for you. We're open pretty much from sunup till sundown, so you can come whenever you like."

"I don't need a reservation?"

Blue eyes glittered as he looked up from a forest of black lashes. "Nah, it's not that kind of place."

She watched his hands, covered in dirt and oil, thumb through the worn wallet, and she noticed a small emblem on one corner of the leather, a gold cross. The symbol reminded her of the main theme of his letters.

I want a bride who loves the Lord more than she loves me.

The statement had caught Destiny unaware, shocked her a little. She didn't have that kind of faith, didn't really understand it, but the guy wrote about it so much that she honestly believed he meant those words. And that intrigued her even more.

"I know I have them in here somewhere."

As he searched for the card, Destiny took the chance to look at his face, and she realized with surprise that it was also fairly well covered with dirt and grime, and one thick smear of what she guessed to be oil across his forehead. Funny, she hadn't even noticed it before. His features had apparently drawn her attention to the important things. Or maybe it was the words he'd written on those love letters that hid any imperfections.

"Here it is." He withdrew the card and handed it to Destiny. "You'll have to excuse the smudge." He pointed to a black smear along the edge. "You can still read the important stuff. And there's another business on the back."

Destiny flipped the card and saw the contact information for the Bowers' Sporting Goods Shop on the Claremont square.

"My grandparents thought it'd be smart to consolidate their two businesses on one card."

"Sounds like a good idea." She tucked the card inside her purse.

The gas pump made a loud racket as it screeched

to a stop. "Looks like it's done." He moved the nozzle from the tank to the pump. "Took fifty-three dollars' worth."

She fished three twenties from her wallet and placed them in his palm.

"Hold on, I'll get your change." He turned and walked toward the station where Bo and Maura quickly jerked their attention from the gas pumps to something else at the counter.

Destiny's cell phone rang. She glanced at the display, saw her managing editor's name, then answered. "Everything okay with today's blog?"

The magazine's website ran an original blog post each day. Usually Destiny wrote the material, but Rita had taken on today's so Destiny could get on the road sooner. Plus, since their entire staff consisted of merely the two of them, if Destiny didn't do it, Rita did. Destiny may have footed the start-up expenses and therefore held the "owner" title, but Rita cared just as much about the magazine's success. Hopefully, if Destiny could keep her advertisers and subscribers happy, she'd one day be able to pay her friend a salary worthy of her efforts.

"Of course, everything's fine," Rita said. "I told you I can handle things."

Destiny grinned. "Okay, so why are you calling?"

"To find out if you met him yet, naturally. Have you? And does he look as good as he sounds on paper?"

"No, he looks better."

"You don't say? Well, maybe I should've been the one to volunteer for this road trip. Then again, it may be a moot point. His grandmother just called again to make sure we weren't publishing his letters and also asked for us to return the originals."

Destiny frowned. Troy's grandmother had entered several of his love letters in the magazine's first Love Letter Contest, and his had blown all of the other entries out of the water. Then, when they'd phoned the lady to let her know she'd won, she admitted she didn't have her grandson's permission to share them. Rita had offered to call and talk to Troy, but the woman had said she'd try to get his permission. When that didn't happen quickly, Destiny decided to head to Alabama herself and request it personally. "Did she say anything else?"

"That Troy had told her specifically today that he didn't want anyone but his future bride seeing those letters and that she wanted to make sure we gave the prize money to whoever came in second…and returned those letters. She said she wants to put them back where she found them before he realizes they're missing."

"None of those other letters even held a candle to his, Rita. You know that. And we promised our advertisers a sneak peek into the heart of a true Southern gentleman. Obviously, there aren't that many of them left, and we've found a winner. I'm not giving up on getting his permission to publish them."

Rita's laugh echoed through the phone. "I thought you'd say that, but I figured you'd want to know what she said. We still need to mail those letters to her, you know."

Destiny glanced at the letters that she'd read and

reread continually ever since they'd arrived in their PO box. Funny, she felt almost territorial about them, as though they were written to her or something. But they weren't, and his grandmother wanted to return them to where she had found them. "Okay. We'll send them back," she said regretfully.

Troy exited the station and started toward her car.

"Hey, he's coming this way. Call you back later." She hung up and tossed the cell back in her purse.

"Here you go." He placed the bills in her hand, and the simple gesture sent a ripple of awareness up her arm. "So, did you have any other questions?"

"Other questions?" She folded the cash and placed it in the console. "Oh, yes, I do. I need to find the Claremont Bed and Breakfast. Could you tell me where it's located?"

"Sure, you keep heading down Claremont-Stockville Road, the way you're going, and you'll run right into the town square. Head to the opposite side and take the road to Maple Street. It's a block down on the left. It's an antebellum plantation, white with double porches all the way around, one on the top floor and the other surrounding the bottom. You can't miss it. Nice place. L. E. and Annette Tingle run it. They're good folks. They'll take care of you."

"Thanks." She didn't make any effort to start the engine. She really didn't want to leave him, but she couldn't think of another reason to stay.

"But that wasn't what I meant." His relaxed and easy tone highlighted his contentment in his world, even if he hadn't found the woman he'd written to for, oh, fifteen years.

"Wasn't what you meant? *What* wasn't what you meant?"

"I was asking if you have any other questions about small-town living. Maybe I could help you out, beyond just showing you how to fish this weekend. Assuming you visit the fishing hole." He grinned. "Anyway, ask away. You're our only customer for the time being. Might as well take advantage of a few minutes to ask small-town questions of the small-town guy."

She racked her brain for every line of those beautifully written letters, and she suddenly knew exactly what to ask in her quest to begin winning Troy's trust. "Just one more question, for now."

"What's that?"

"It's Wednesday, and I'd love to attend a midweek worship. Can you tell me if there's a church in town that I could visit tonight?" She couldn't remember the last time she'd graced a church for a midweek service. In fact, she missed more Sundays than she attended, but she did find her way to church every now and again. And this morning, she'd even found her Bible and packed it for the trip because faith was important to Troy. So for now she'd find hers again, too. Never hurt to spend time in church; she just rarely found the time to make the effort. But she'd make it now.

He hesitated, then one corner of his mouth kicked up a notch, and that dimple made a reappearance. "Sure, Claremont Community Church has a midweek worship. And it's pretty easy to find. There's a sign for the church at the end of a road a little ways before you get to the square. You can't miss it. Worship starts at seven."

A little ways. The quaint term sounded adorable, especially when delivered with that deep drawl. Instead of asking him exactly how far that constituted, she said, "Sounds great." She turned the key. "And will you be there?"

"I try to never miss."

"Then I'll see you there." She gave him her best smile and a small wave, and then drove away from the guy she'd planned to meet ever since her magazine received that batch of letters from his grandmother last month. And she'd seen it in his eyes: her church question took him by pleasant surprise. Good. She wanted to convince him to trust her, be her friend and eventually agree to help save her magazine. Perhaps in the process, he'd get his own version of her magazine's name.

Southern Love.

Chapter Two

Today I saw a vision of what I want for us in the future. Maura packed a picnic lunch for Bo, and the two of them sat behind the service station while I ran the place and they enjoyed their quiet time. I look forward to having quiet time with you, time to reflect on our day, time to reflect on our faith. I look forward to many years sharing quiet time and enjoying each other's company, building our love together and coming to know each other so well that we can read each other's thoughts without words.

Troy folded the letter and placed it in the wooden box that held the most recent of the letters that he'd written for the past fifteen years. The thing was, his grandmother had struck a nerve today with her impromptu visit to the station. He hadn't anticipated passing his twenty-seventh birthday and still not finding the recipient of these letters. Then again, he asked God to send her in His time, so he knew that the Lord would put the right woman in his life one day. Maybe this weekend's date with Haley Calhoun would be the start of something that would last longer than a date or two.

His mind flashed to Destiny Porter, the woman who'd come by the station today. Silky chocolate hair and bright blue eyes in a pretty heart-shaped face. She wasn't overly made-up and didn't appear fake like a lot of girls he knew. Then again, they only seemed fake when they started the bizarre flirting that Troy couldn't stand. He wanted a woman who spoke from the heart, and he hadn't found that yet. But this woman, Destiny Porter, had seemed undeniably real. However, she was only passing through, here for a while to write about small-town living. She had big city written all over her, from the snazzy clothes she wore to the flashy car she drove.

No, he couldn't see himself dating someone like that, but he had found her easy to talk to. And she'd asked about church, not merely church on Sunday but the midweek service. She was visiting from out of town and still took initiative to find a church for worship in the middle of the week.

Troy couldn't deny he'd been impressed on several levels. Her natural appearance, pretty but not overdone. Her interest in faith, genuine and without putting on a show. And the easy way she'd talked to him, looked at him, seemed comfortable with him.

He glanced back at the wooden box. Those were qualities he'd described several times over the years, a woman who was real, a woman who had faith and a woman he could relate to easily. He'd met Haley at church Sunday morning, and she'd seemed right at home talking about faith and God, even if she'd had to rush out after church when she'd gotten a call about a sick calf. Luckily, he'd already asked her if she'd like to have dinner Friday before she got that call.

He left his house and drove to the church wondering if he'd see the new vet at tonight's service. Turning onto the parking lot, he immediately spotted Destiny's bright red convertible parked beneath a huge magnolia. She leaned against the side of the car, a Bible tucked beneath her arm, and the setting sun highlighted her there, smiling at Troy as she held up a hand.

She wore a pale blue sundress with a white sweater and white sandals, her brown hair pulled into a low ponytail on the side, the same way it'd been when he saw her at the station. Like earlier today, she had a natural girl-next-door quality that Troy found appealing. He found himself wondering if she had a guy back in Atlanta, then shook the thought away. She was in a different league, lived a different life than small-town Claremont, and Haley had the very same qualities, pretty and natural and real, but she lived here and admittedly loved small-town living. Troy should keep his focus on the girl he'd go out with in two nights.

But there was no harm in helping the city girl with her story. He pulled his truck in next to her car, grabbed his Bible off the seat and climbed out. "So you found the church okay?"

"Yes, and thanks, your directions were spot-on." She lifted her shoulders a little as she spoke, and Troy noticed the thin line of pearls circling her slender neck. Matching tiny pearl earrings dotted each ear, and again he thought about how much he liked her simple yet elegant taste. Her look wasn't over the top, but it was very feminine.

"Well, I'm glad you made it here okay."

"I hope you don't mind, but I kind of waited for you." Her smile was shy, sweet, and Troy found himself returning the gesture easily.

"You waited for me?"

"I knew you said you were coming and, I know this sounds crazy, but I get a little nervous when I go somewhere for the first time. I guess it's that first-day-of-school type feeling, where you don't know anyone and are hesitant about how you'll fit in."

He knew the feeling well and remembered each time he'd experienced it. "First day of school, first day on a job, first date with a girl," he said, grinning when he thought about how many of those he'd had, "or in your case, with a guy."

She laughed, and he liked the way even her laughter seemed real, natural, right. "Yes, that's it. First-day jitters. I was hoping you wouldn't mind showing me around, maybe letting me know where the classrooms are, or does everyone meet in the auditorium on Wednesdays?"

"We have a few different classes, the youth, singles, young marrieds, middle marrieds, new parents, those types of things."

She looked surprised. "Wow, that's a lot of options."

"Yeah, we have quite a few, but there aren't that many people in each group. Claremont's a small town, you know, but the folks at church like their Wednesday night study groups to cover applicable topics."

"So do you go to the singles class?"

"Nah." He glanced around for the pale blue pickup that Haley had driven on Sunday but didn't spot it in the parking lot.

"Looking for someone?"

"Yeah, but I guess she didn't make it this evening. You ready to go in?"

"I am." She walked beside him toward the building. "So what class do you go to?"

"I usually go in the auditorium for Brother Henry's lesson with the main group. Truth is, it's mostly all of the elderly members of the congregation." He waited to see if she'd ask why he'd selected that group, and he wasn't all that certain how he'd explain the choice. *Because I've dated everyone in the singles class, and I'm not married yet, so young marrieds and middle marrieds won't exactly fly.* Somehow that answer didn't seem best. Thankfully, she didn't ask, so he didn't have to worry about how to respond.

"Could I go with you to that one then, since I'll know someone there?"

"Sure. Bo and Maura, the couple that you met this afternoon who own the service station, will be in the class. And the Tingles, who own the bed-and-breakfast where you're staying, will be there, too. So you'll actually know a few."

"I can feel those first-day jitters going away already."

He opened the door for her when they reached the top of the church steps. She passed near him, smiled and thanked him. And Troy found himself inhaling her faintly floral scent, not a perfume that overpowered his senses, but a pleasing fresh fragrance.

She responded to the greeters inside the lobby, and he noticed how easily she chatted and exchanged small talk with Bryant and Anna Bowman, the older couple assigned to welcoming everyone this evening. If she did feel the first-day jitters, or like a fish out of water, in the small community church, it didn't show. In fact, she looked very much at ease making her way through the lobby with Troy introducing her to those still visiting before class.

By the time they reached the auditorium, Brother Henry was getting ready to pray. Troy directed her to his regular pew, midway from the front and in the center of the church. He saw a few church members take an unhidden interest in the woman situating herself on the pew beside Troy. Most noticeable were his mother and grandmother, sitting together as usual in the second row. No, they shouldn't have turned around and gawked at Troy when he came in, but that was their nature. And it took his grandfather and father tapping their shoulders before they turned around. Of course, his grandfather and father also stared at the pretty girl by his side.

Troy sent his dad a subtle shake of his head to make sure he'd get the hint that this wasn't anything more than him sitting with the newcomer. Hopefully his dad would fill his mother and grandparents in before church ended and they were stuck to Ms. Porter like white on rice.

As was typical with the Wednesday night service, Brother Henry moved around the room and offered each member in attendance a chance to read the next passage in their class material or the next Bible verse.

Troy noticed Destiny having a difficult time locating Philippians, and when it neared her time to read, he leaned over and touched her Bible.

"Want me to help you find it?"

Her cheeks blushed pink, and he was afraid he'd embarrassed her.

"I noticed you're using a new Bible, so I'm sure you're probably still learning where everything's located in that one. Amazing how a different font or a translation can do that, huh?" He kept his voice as low as possible so as not to disturb the other class members and also so he wouldn't point out the fact that she was having a hard time.

Her look of embarrassment all but disappeared. "Yes, thanks."

"You want to take the next one, Troy?" Brother Henry's voice took their attention off each other and back to the study.

Troy read the verse. As soon as he finished, he flipped to the next verse in Destiny's Bible, so she was ready when Brother Henry asked if she'd like to read.

When the class ended, Troy wasn't surprised to see his mother and grandmother making a beeline for his pew. He knew better than to try to leave; they'd just chase him down in the parking lot.

"Mom, Grandma, this is Destiny. She's visiting from Atlanta."

"Really? You don't say." His mother's ambitious nod and smile went overboard. Troy knew she was ready for him to find the right one, but she could stand to tone down the look of hope at him merely standing beside the visiting lady.

But his mother's look had nothing on his grand-mother's. Jolaine Bowers's blue eyes were so wide, her smile so bright, that Troy wouldn't be at all sur-prised if she didn't start clapping and tell him that it was high time he gave her some great-grandchildren, and that she thought Destiny perfect for the job. Then her head tilted, and she looked confused. "Destiny? I thought your name was Haley. Haley Calhoun."

"Haley didn't make it tonight," Troy said.

Her brows shot up with such force they nearly dis-appeared beneath her bangs. "I thought our talk today helped you." She attempted to whisper, but people in the lobby probably heard.

"Destiny is visiting town to write a story, and I of-fered to help. She also asked where to attend a mid-week Bible study, so I told her, and she came." Troy picked up his Bible from the pew and waited for the interrogation to continue.

His grandmother didn't disappoint. "So you're still going out with Haley on Friday?" She looked to Des-tiny. "I'm sorry, dear, but we're working on the fact that my grandson has been labeled a player."

"Mother, really." Troy's mom shook her head. "For-give my mom," she said to Destiny, "I'm afraid she's long since lost her filter for what information to share and what she should keep to herself."

"The whole town knows it," his grandmother said. "Just go to the beauty shop and ask them. Or the quilt-ing group. Or our online loop."

Troy could tell Destiny didn't know how to re-spond, and he grinned. "My grandmother's defini-tion of a player and the one you're thinking of probably don't coincide, but for now, I won't try to explain." He edged toward his grandmother, hugged her and lowered his voice. "I appreciate you attempting to help me out, but I think I've got this. I'm still going out with Haley on Friday, but I believe I can help Ms. Porter write her story on small-town living, too."

She huffed out a breath. "If you say so." But then she seemed to focus on the positive aspect of Destiny's occupation. "Wait, you're a writer? You write for newspapers, magazines? Or do you write books?" Her look of admiration grew along with the size of the publications she listed. "Are you a bestseller or something like that?" Her head bobbed and she appeared a bit starstruck. "Have you written anything that we might find at A Likely Story?"

"A Likely Story?" Destiny asked, handling this grilling fairly well, in Troy's opinion. He'd have to apologize profusely later, if he ever got her away from his mother and grandmother.

"A Likely Story is our local bookstore, on the town square," his mother explained. "It's been here since I was a little girl, and it's adorable. You have to visit the store while you're in town."

"Oh, yes, you must visit," his grandmother continued. "Maybe we could set up a book signing for you there. Do you have any recent releases? I'll make sure to ask David Presley, the store owner, to order plenty of your books."

"No relation," Troy's mother said.

"Relation?" Destiny asked.

"To Elvis, of course," his grandmother explained, and Troy began to think that he probably owed this woman more than an apology, maybe a cup of coffee or even dinner, for what his mother and grandmother were putting her through right now. But that'd qualify as a date, and he'd already asked out Haley Calhoun. No need to feed his player reputation by asking the writer out, too. But if his grandmother didn't back down, she might ditch her story on small-town living. Or title it "The Twilight Zone" and sell it to a sci-fi mag. "And we can put it in the church bulletin announcements. When would you like to have your signing, dear?"

He could tell Destiny didn't know how to answer his eccentric family's questions, so he decided to help her out. "She said she's writing a story about small towns," he explained. "I'm pretty sure that means she's writing for a newspaper or maybe a magazine. Probably not a novelist, are you, Destiny?"

Her cheeks lifted with her smile and made her eyes appear a more brilliant blue within the long, dark lashes. "That's right, I'm not." And then, at his grandmother's obvious look of disappointment, she added, "But I've always dreamed about writing a book. Maybe I'll try it one day."

Grandma's grin reclaimed her face. "Well, that sounds wonderful, just wonderful. You should write one about Claremont, definitely. It's a small town, but *plenty* goes on in a small town, let me tell you."

Troy feared that she might start telling her all about the plenty going on, courtesy of her time today at the beauty shop. "Grandma, I'm going to walk Destiny out to her car." He knew if he left without Destiny, the questioning would continue, and he could only imagine what they'd ask if he wasn't standing nearby. "I'll see you at the fishing hole on Saturday."

"Would you like to come to the fishing hole, too, Destiny?" his grandmother asked. "It's really a lot nicer than it sounds. James and I have been fixing the place up for years, and it's almost as pretty as Hydrangea Park. It'd make a good addition to your story. I'll fix you some of my famous chicken fingers while you're there. And a chocolate pie. Maybe some of my peach delight. I bet you haven't had peach delight before."

"I'm sure she'd love your peach delight, Mama, but she probably needs to leave. The church is nearly empty." Troy's mother wrapped an arm around his grandmother and kissed her cheek. He loved them both dearly, even if they did tend to meddle a little—or a lot—more than they should.

"Aw, thanks, dear. Well, maybe Destiny could put the fishing hole in her book." She gave another look of hope, and this one had nothing to do with eliminating Troy's player status and everything to do with advertising. "What do you think?"

"When I write the book, I just might," Destiny said, and Troy commended her silently for appeasing his precious, albeit determined, grandmother.

They walked toward the lobby, the crowd thinning as everyone made their way home, and Troy noticed the straight white-blond hair that had first caught his attention Sunday morning. The new veterinarian stood at the church doorway chatting with Brother Henry. "Haley?"

She turned and smiled. "Hey."

Troy took the few steps to close the distance between them. "I figured you didn't make it to the service."

"I put on a watch that I'd forgotten to change from Eastern to Central time and actually showed up an hour early. Then I left when I got a call from John Cutter about his mare getting sick. And by the time I got done there and cleaned up, I was late to church." She laughed. "Seems I can't ever get my timing right."

"That's okay," Brother Henry said. "We're glad you made it. Which class did you attend?"

"The singles class, and I enjoyed it very much."

"Maybe you should attend that class again, Troy." His grandmother had naturally been eavesdropping and jumped into the conversation. "I'm Jolaine Bowers, Troy's grandmother. So you're Haley Calhoun? The new vet?"

Haley nodded. "Yes, I am. It's nice to meet you." She extended her hand.

"Wonderful to meet you," his grandmother said, taking Haley's hand and then squeezing it. "My, you sure are pretty, aren't you? Don't you think so, Troy?"

Troy said a quick prayer that his grandmother would let up. "Yes," he said, then when he was certain his grandmother had looked away, he mouthed to Haley, "Sorry."

She laughed softly, and he liked the sound. Then she looked from Troy to Destiny, still standing nearby.

Troy mentally slapped himself for forgetting the natural introduction. "Haley, this is Destiny. She's visiting Claremont from Atlanta and writing about small-town living. She came by the station today, and

I offered to help her with her story. Then I told her about the church service tonight, and she came." Why did he feel like he was giving an explanation of his normal actions?

Luckily, neither girl looked as though his clarification sounded odd, but he caught his grandmother's brow lift and knew she could tell he was, for some reason, uncomfortable.

"I think a story about Claremont would be very interesting. I moved here last week from Ocala, Florida. The lifestyle is so different here. Everyone knows everyone." She grinned. "They even know each other's pets."

"Maybe I could talk to you about the differences between Ocala and Claremont," Destiny said, then added, "for my story."

"That'd be great."

"I'm going to head back to the bed-and-breakfast." Destiny looked to Brother Henry. "I enjoyed your lesson."

"Thank you. I hope we'll see you again while you're in town."

She glanced toward Troy, then Haley, and answered, "You will."

Troy said goodbye and watched her leave, then he chatted awhile with Haley about her day and about the plans he had for their upcoming date. She was easy to talk to, naturally pretty, obviously loved God and had a strong faith. But Troy couldn't deny that while he talked to the attractive vet, looked into her deep green eyes, he kept thinking about the woman who'd sat beside him in class, let him help her navigate the new Bible and kept his interest throughout the day.

Troy swallowed, put the image of bright blue eyes away and focused on trying not to live up to his player classification. "I'm looking forward to Friday, too," he said, while out of the corner of his eye, he watched the red Beemer drive away.

Chapter Three

"You do realize I don't expect you to work on the holiday." Destiny hit the speaker button and placed her cell phone on the white wicker table beside her rocking chair on the B and B's porch. She'd been out here writing and surfing the internet most of the day, but she hadn't expected Rita to spend her Fourth of July away from fun, too.

"I know that, and I've been at Lake Lanier all morning with my family. Just thought I'd check emails this afternoon before we head to the fireworks in Gwinnett County tonight."

Destiny took a sip of Annette Tingle's delicious fresh-squeezed lemonade. She imagined a lot of families spent the day together on lakes or beaches or merely visiting in the family home. Her own family had gathered for a barbecue, according to one of the many text messages her mother had sent throughout the day. The majority of the texts, of course, reminded Destiny that she was chasing a pipe dream and told her she should be in Atlanta with her family and spending her time finding a real job. And as if the text messages weren't enough...

"Hey, did your mother ever get hold of you?"

The sweet lemonade suddenly turned bitter. Destiny placed the cool glass on the table and took the phone off speaker in case Mr. or Mrs. Tingle came outside. She didn't need to share her family's discontent with the world. "Did Mama call you?"

"Just a couple of times. Mostly she sent texts. Oh, and here's a couple of emails from her in my in-box."

Destiny's jaw tensed, and she consciously forced it to relax before she chipped a tooth. "I'm so sorry. I should've known she wouldn't have been satisfied with my responses to her texts."

"How'd you respond?"

"Same way I always respond. I told her I'm fine." Destiny heard the front door creak open and turned to see Mr. Tingle heading out with more red, white and blue bunting for the porch railing. Mrs. Tingle followed, opened her mouth to say hello but then closed it when she saw Destiny on the phone, and gave her a polite finger wave as they went about hanging even more decorations. They'd already lined the sidewalk with tiny American flags, placed planters filled with red, white and blue flowers on every porch step and draped each bush with patriotic twinkle lights. And they weren't finished yet.

"That's it? You texted that you're fine?" Rita didn't do a very good job at muffling her laugh. "So I'm guessing she's now totally convinced that you aren't fine, right? Back in college, she'd have already driven over to figure out exactly what was wrong." Before becoming Destiny's pitifully paid but devoted managing editor, Rita had been her best friend through high school and her roommate in college. And during those years at the University of Georgia, she got a full taste of Geneva Porter's persistence.

Destiny's phone buzzed with an incoming text, and she didn't bother checking the sender. No doubt her mom's persistence was still in full force. "She never thinks I'm fine, because if I'm not doing exactly what she has planned for my life, then I'm obviously doomed." Destiny noticed the Tingles exchange a look as they hung the next section of bunting and realized her voice easily carried across the porch. She smiled at the sweet couple, and Mrs. Tingle smiled back, but there was a hint of pity in her eyes.

Destiny smiled brighter, determined to convince someone today that she really was fine. "The decorations look amazing," she said to the pair.

"Why, thank you, dear. L.E. is a real champ helping me decorate everything for the holidays. You should see this place at Christmas." She leaned toward her husband and kissed his cheek.

Destiny may not have ever found love herself, but she knew it when she saw it, and she made a mental note to write the Tingles' love story for her magazine before she headed back to Atlanta.

"The town is decorated for the Fourth?" Rita asked, reminding Destiny that her friend was still on the line.

"Yeah, every house on Maple Street looks like a cake decorated with red, white and blue icing."

Mr. Tingle, obviously hearing her description, nodded as though that were an accurate assessment, and

Mrs. Tingle followed suit. They were so content, so undeniably happy running the bed-and-breakfast together. Destiny wondered what that'd be like, to "fit" so well with someone that even regular daily activities became a joy because you were together.

She'd never known that. And truthfully, she'd never seen that in her own home. Her mother, quite frankly, didn't seem to be happy unless she was miserable. Or making someone else miserable, namely Destiny. Her sister, Beverly, however, did no wrong. Destiny loved her younger sis, even if her mom did play favorites and she'd come up with the short straw.

"Oh, just got another text from your mom. She's asking me if you've talked to your sister today."

Destiny closed her eyes, counted to five—if she went to ten, she'd just miss another text from her mom—then said, "Something must be up. I'll call you back later. Let me figure out what's going on with Mom."

"Good luck with that."

Destiny smiled and was grateful that her friend was able to afford her that luxury. "Yeah, I know. You go have fun and enjoy the fireworks, and tell your family I said hello."

"I will, but promise me you'll do the same. There's gotta be something fun to do there if they're decorating the place so much. Maybe Claremont, Alabama, will top the Gwinnett fireworks display."

Destiny doubted the small town did all that much for the holiday, but if the decorations on Maple Street were any indication, they went all out as much as they could. "I'll see what's going on."

"And you'll actually join in the fun?" Rita asked. "That's part of your problem, you know, you work too much and don't get out to enjoy life. Who knows, you may actually meet Mr. Right down there." Then before allowing Destiny to provide her trademark answer, that she didn't believe such a man existed, at least not for her, Rita added, "Hey, what about Troy Lee?"

"What about him?" Surely her friend wasn't suggesting that the country boy with the tender heart was Destiny's Mr. Right. Because that would never work, ever. The only reason she wanted to even meet the guy was to get his permission to run his love letters. She'd never take an interest in him herself.

Vivid blue eyes within a sea of black lashes suddenly flashed into her mind, along with that deadly dimple. And the fact that he was so solidly grounded in his faith. That rich baritone reading the Bible verses in church last night had given her chills, and in a good way. He hadn't been putting on a show at church; he'd believed every word he read in those Bible scriptures about rejoicing. And listening to him, Destiny had found herself yearning to feel that way, to experience that faith, to find that kind of contentment. In fact, she'd thought about the Bible lesson several times throughout the day and about how Troy truly seemed to have the joy mentioned in those scriptures.

She'd never had that kind of joy, or that kind of faith, which emphasized how different her background was from Troy's. And then there was his family. She'd read lots about them in his letters and how he wanted a family like that one day—big and boisterous and happy. Destiny couldn't imagine a family like that for herself. No, she and a guy like Troy Lee would never mesh.

"Did you see him today?" Rita continued. "You said you were going to try to talk to him again at the filling station, didn't you?"

"Yeah, I'd planned to, but I wasn't thinking about today being a holiday. I rode over early this morning, but it was closed." Then she'd come back and camped out on this porch all day. Oddly, she hadn't felt bored. The scene was too pretty not to enjoy every minute, and she'd gotten a good deal of writing done for her next few blog posts, primarily focusing on Southern charm and the way all Southerners enjoy a reason to celebrate. She wondered how Troy was celebrating. "I'm going to try to see him tomorrow."

"Think he'll give you permission to run the letters? We had another batch of emails from subscribers asking when they'd get to read some of the love letters you promised in last month's issue. I think they're wanting some sort of teaser."

"Well, the teaser was when I said we'd have them this month. That's as good as I can do until I gain the rights to publish." And she had to gain Troy Lee's trust first, which meant spending time with him, but there hadn't been a way to make that happen today. According to his grandmother, he had no desire whatsoever to share his private letters with the world. Destiny had to somehow change his mind.

"Maybe you should write about him in your blog posts, that you've met him and all. Describe him to your readers so they can get to know the man whose letters they'll read in the next issue."

"That's a good idea. And I'll go back to the filling station tomorrow, and then I'll go to the fishing hole on Saturday. Should be able to spend some time with him both days." And she also knew how to see him on Sunday: by making another appearance at church. Funny, she found herself looking forward to visiting the small congregation again.

"Well..." Rita drew out the word. "Maybe he's *your* Mr. Right."

Destiny controlled the tone of her response to hide any indication that she'd discounted that very thought not five minutes ago. "You're dreaming big today, aren't you?"

"They say opposites attract."

Destiny wondered how many opposites Rita noticed when she thought of herself and Troy. Let's see, there was the faith thing; that was one. A big, happy family; that was two. Honest and trustworthy; a big fat three and four.

She shook the thought—and all of the many opposites, which, she assumed, could pile up quick if she kept counting—and decided to nip this conversation in the bud before Rita got carried away with the crazy notion. "He's dating someone." That wasn't actually true, since from what his grandmother said at church his first official date with Haley Calhoun was tomorrow night. But the two had looked quite beautiful together when Destiny left them talking at the church. And that was close enough to dating; plus, it'd get Rita off her back.

"Aw, that's a shame."

"I write about the good guys and the potential that

they actually exist. I don't pretend to believe that one will ever be a part of my world. For me, it's the bad experiences that ring true. I'll just keep writing about those, when it comes to my love life." She forced a laugh. "I sure have plenty of material to work with."

"Bless your heart." Annette Tingle's whispered words came from the other side of the porch railing, where she and L.E. continued tacking up the bunting, and Destiny was once again reminded how her voice carried.

"No, really, it's okay," she said to the sweet lady, and gave her another smile that must've come off as pretty fake, judging from the way Mrs. Tingle still shook her head.

Another text buzzed in on the line, and Destiny wrapped up the conversation. "Mom's still trying to get me. I've gotta let you go."

"Okay, but I'm not hanging up until you promise you'll have some fun before the day ends."

Destiny laughed, a real one this time. "I'll have some fun."

"You'll have some fun *today.* Say it."

"I promise I'll have some fun today." She looked up in time to see both of the Tingles nodding.

"We'll get you an itinerary of tonight's activities on the town square. Claremont really pulls out all the stops for holidays," Mr. Tingle said.

"I heard that," Rita chirped through the line. "And if they 'pull out all the stops,' then there should be something you can do to have a good time and forget about work."

Destiny grinned. "I'm sure you're right." She really

did need to get her mind off the magazine for a little while. The toll of knowing the majority of her advertisers threatened to pull out if she didn't get her subscription numbers up was wearing her down.

If she hadn't sunk almost all of her savings into starting and then advertising it, and if she didn't have to listen to her mother tell her every day of her life how unwise a move that was, maybe it'd be a little easier to relax and have fun every now and then. Plus, there was Rita. Destiny's friend had believed in the idea from the get-go and worked as hard as Destiny to make it shine. If Destiny could get her numbers up and gain those subscriptions and advertisers, she'd finally be able to pay Rita the type of salary she deserved. Rita was such a great friend, even calling on her holiday to make sure Destiny had some fun.

The phone buzzed with yet another text message.

No doubt Destiny wouldn't be allowed to have fun until her mother was appeased. "Talk to you later, Rita." She disconnected then scanned the list of missed calls and texts.

Shockingly enough, not all of them were from her mother. Half were from Beverly. And as Destiny wondered which person to call first, the phone rang. Thankfully, it was her sister. She clicked the call button.

"Hey, Bevvie, what's going on?"

"Has Mom called you? Have you talked to her yet? I told her to let me talk to you first, but I know how hard it is for her to keep anything to herself." Her sister's voice was breathless, as though she'd just finished the Peachtree Marathon or something. Which, come to think of it, the annual marathon *had* been this morning, and Bevvie usually ran in the event.

"Oh, wow, did you win the Peachtree?"

Beverly's laughter rolled through the line. "No, silly, I didn't even run. I'd planned to, but Jared wanted me to go with him this morning to Stone Mountain. We hiked to the top and watched the most amazing sunrise I've ever seen. Oh, Destiny, it was so beautiful."

The happiness in her sister's voice pierced Destiny's heart a little, not because she was jealous of what Bevvie had found with Jared, but because she doubted she'd ever sound—or feel—that happy. How many guys had broken Destiny's heart? Oh, right, she'd stopped counting after five. "That sounds nice, Bev."

"Oh, it was so much better than nice, Destiny. I'm so happy! And I'm glad I'm getting to tell you before Mom. You haven't talked to her yet, have you?"

The phone buzzed, and Destiny didn't check the display to verify that her mother was still going at it. "Not yet, but I think she's still trying to get through."

"Awesome, then I get to tell you the news. Jared asked me to marry him this morning, as the sun came up. Marry him! Destiny, I'm engaged! Can you believe it? Engaged! And we're going to have a short engagement, planning to get married on Christmas Eve. Won't that be great? I want you to be my maid of honor, of course. You will, won't you?"

Destiny blinked a couple of times. "Of course." She swallowed, gathered her bearings. Her little sister, three years younger, had a great job, a super guy and an engagement ring on her finger.

"I've been waiting to put the pictures on Facebook until I talk to you, but you'll be able to see them soon. Mom took them. Can you believe that? After Jared asked Daddy for my hand—wow, it's so exciting saying that!—anyway, after that, then he asked Mom and Dad if they could hike the mountain early this morning so they could witness everything and take the photos. I didn't even see them up there, but they were watching and saw everything. Dad even cried."

Their mother always sported a camera and loved taking photographs, though Destiny was sure taking engagement pictures of their daughter topped any other photo op. "I'm happy for you, Bevvie." And she meant it. She was happy. Which really didn't make sense with the tears dripping solidly down her cheeks. They traced a path along her jaw and down her throat, and Destiny didn't bother wiping them away.

A tissue materialized in front of her face, and she looked up to see Mrs. Tingle handing her an entire box. She forced a smile, mouthed "thanks," and then continued to listen to Beverly discuss everything about her morning and her plans for the wedding while Destiny swiped at her cheeks, jaw and throat. "The entire church will be decorated snow-white and accented by crimson poinsettias. I think we'll use a lot of those little twinkle lights, too. But a lot of that will be up to the wedding coordinator, or wedding planner, whatever you call it. Mom says we're getting the best, one of her friends from the country club. Can you believe it?"

Destiny imagined all of the plans their mother had

already started. Finally, a daughter getting married. Definitely cause for a Geneva Porter celebration. "It'll be gorgeous, Bevvie. I can't wait."

"Me either!"

Destiny took a deep breath, lifted the Fourth of July itinerary from where Mrs. Tingle had placed it on the table by her lemonade and box of tissues, and saw that the parade would start in an hour. She could use a parade right now. Actually, what she could really use was a ridiculous abundance of ice cream, but a parade would do. "I'm going to check out some of the holiday things going on in Claremont tonight. Give Jared a hug for me and tell him I'm excited to be gaining a brother."

"Oh, I will. I've been hugging him all day, isn't that right, honey?" She laughed as she apparently distributed another hug to her boyfriend—correction—fiancé. "Love you, sis!"

Destiny closed her eyes and prayed that the tears slipping beneath her lashes were the last of them. "Love you right back." She heard the line click as Bevvie, still laughing, disconnected, then opened her eyes and saw she'd missed two more texts from her mom. Rather than attempt a conversation with her right now, when she knew her mother would pick up on her tiny pity party, she sent a simple text.

Bevvie called with her news. So happy for her! Can't wait for her big day.

Then she powered down the phone, finished her lemonade and decided that one way or another, she was going to follow Rita's instructions and enjoy the rest of her day. Starting with a parade.

Troy loved the Fourth of July. His family always got into holiday gatherings, but the Fourth was especially fun because Claremont had so much to offer for the big day. They'd started out the morning at the fishing hole with the annual family fishing competition. The youngest member of the group, Troy's three-year-old niece, Lily, won...with a little help from Troy, handing her his fishing rod whenever he caught a fish, while the remainder of the family pretended not to notice and Lily did her best to keep the secret. It was almost as much fun watching the little girl try to contain her giggles as it was to see everyone cheer for her accomplishment each time she "caught" another fish.

Next they'd eaten enough of his grandmother's crispy fried chicken fingers, creamy potato salad, buttery corn on the cob and every other traditional fixing she'd prepared, then followed that with a family Bible study by the lake. After a little more fishing, a refreshing swim and then quite a few family members taking naps on quilts by the water while Troy and his brothers played a fairly intense round of ultimate Frisbee, the entire group cleaned up and gathered again at the town square for Claremont's night of "Fun on the Fourth."

Troy's four younger brothers, ranging in age from fourteen to twenty-one, were already involved in an impromptu game of tag football with some other guys their age while the town waited for the parade to start. At twenty-seven, Troy was older than the group, so he didn't join in. He still liked sports, but the guys his age didn't typically hog the large grassy area near the center of the square the way they did when they were teens. Most, in fact, were here with their wives, and some already had kids. However, the "older" gang still got together regularly for their men's baseball league, which Troy enjoyed immensely. But even then, he was usually the odd man out, since the remainder of them had their wives or steady girlfriends in the stands cheering them on.

There was a baseball game scheduled for Sunday afternoon. Maybe, if tomorrow night's date went well, he'd see if Haley wanted to come. He'd texted her earlier and asked if she'd be attending the parade tonight, and she'd responded that she was catching up on some paperwork but that she'd try. He let her know that his family would watch the parade in front of the Sweet Stop candy shop, same place they camped out every year for the event. Scanning the area beneath the red-and-white-striped awning that identified the store, he didn't see any sign of the pretty blonde. He'd keep an eye out for her, though, because it wouldn't hurt to spend a little time with her tonight. A "pre-date" date, so to speak. And it'd give his family a chance to get to know the girl he planned on trying to go out with more than once. Their opinion of his future bride was important, as he'd written in several of his letters over the years. Funny how he suddenly felt as though they'd meet her soon, or maybe had already met her.

Is that feeling coming from You, Lord? Have I finally met her? Would he spend this Fourth of July at the town square watching the parade with his future bride?

"I don't care how many times we come here for the Fourth, it always takes my breath away." Troy's sister, Becca, Lily's mom, smiled brightly as she took in the scene. "I wish Joey could've come with us." Her husband, a Claremont policeman, was on duty tonight and would miss the fun at the square; however, he'd been with the family for fishing and picnicking earlier, so he'd at least participated in some of the family's holiday fun.

Troy and the remainder of the family tried to keep Becca busy whenever Joey pulled night duty. Even though there was little to no crime in Claremont, his sis still got nervous when her husband patrolled at night.

"I'm sure the decorations will still be up tomorrow for the First Friday celebration. Maybe the two of you can bring Lily here for that and he can enjoy the scene then."

"I'd forgotten about tomorrow being First Friday." She nodded. "That's a great idea."

On the first Friday of each month, Claremont held a festival where the local artists and vendors displayed their wares and performed for the town. Everyone came to the event and, while it wasn't the Fourth of July, it would still be a fun activity for Becca to enjoy with her husband. The smile on her face said she agreed.

"And I bet you're right," she said. "They'll keep all the decorations up for tomorrow. Probably the only thing missing will be the fireworks."

"Probably so." Troy took in the scene as well, tiny white lights capping the eaves of every storefront, patriotic ribbons and flags hanging from each window and lamppost, even red, white and blue spotlights showcasing the three-tiered fountain in the center of the square.

The place was always appealing, but especially so on holidays, when all the shop owners brought their merchandise out to the sidewalks and visited with the customers and one another as the entire town joined in the fun. Troy's parents were helping his grandfather welcome customers at Bowers' Sporting Goods, but his grandmother had opted to stay with the remainder of the family, mainly because she loved watching all of the kids enjoy the parade, and she also liked to catch a little candy for herself.

Several local bands, including Troy's favorite Christian group, More Than This, took turns playing on the event's main stage. An abundance of artists had easels set up and were painting outside Gina Brown's Art Gallery, and Troy spotted Gina alongside her protégés. He waved at the sweet lady who, like Troy, attended services at the church every time the doors were open and, with paintbrush in hand, she waved back.

Troy loved Claremont, loved the relationships with the community, the church and his family. He'd always appreciated the small town and planned to raise his own family here one day, assuming he ever found that one person to share his life and love with.

He thought of the letter he wrote this afternoon, tucked away in the wooden box with the remainder of his most recent letters. He'd written so many now that he'd had to store them by year in plastic bins, currently lining one wall of his garage. His family, the only people he'd told of his letter writing, often teased him about the ritual he'd started fifteen years ago, but Troy knew they didn't mean any harm, even his feisty grandmother, whom he'd found going through his letters a couple of months ago.

"Do you think you've set your sights too high?" she'd asked.

The question had haunted him ever since. Had he? Or had God just not brought the right one into his world yet?

A tug at his shirt took his attention from thoughts of his future wife to the pigtailed, black-haired princess who'd been at his side all day, ever since he helped her win that fishing war. "Uncle Troy, can you carry me high? Please?"

Becca shook her head. "Lily, give Uncle Troy a break. He's probably tired."

"Me? Tired?" Troy grinned at his precious niece. "Never." He scooped her up and placed her "high" as she'd requested, which meant, in three-year-old speak, atop his shoulders. She clapped and hugged his head when she got her wish, and Troy laughed in spite of the fact that her exuberant hug yanked his hair. His six-two put her way above the remainder of the crowd, but she seemed to enjoy it and apparently had no fear of heights. "She's going to be a daredevil, I'm thinking."

"That's what I'm afraid of." But Becca's wink and grin said that was fine, as long as Lily was happy. And from the squeals echoing above Troy's head, she was definitely happy.

"You should've invited Haley to the parade." His

grandmother edged her way between Troy and Becca as they joined the rest of the crowd walking around the square. "She may not have known Claremont had a parade tonight, and it'd have been the gentlemanly thing to do for you to invite her." She tsked. "I should've thought of that earlier, so I could've told you to do it."

Becca laughed. "Grandma, how would we ever know what to do if you didn't tell us?"

"I know!" Jolaine Bowers nodded, completely missing the sarcasm in her granddaughter's tone.

Troy grinned. "You'll be proud of me, Grandma. I texted her and invited her to the parade."

"You did?" She scanned the crowd. "So, where is she? Did you tell her where we watch the parade? Maybe she's lost in the crowd. Want me to go look for her? I don't mind, you know."

"No," he chuckled, "I told her where we watch the parade, so she'll meet us at the Sweet Stop if she comes. She didn't say she'd come for sure, just that she'd try."

"She'd *try?* What else would she have to do tonight?"

"Paperwork at the animal hospital."

"It's a holiday. Didn't you tell her?"

"See now, there's where I went wrong. I invited her to the Fourth of July parade, but completely forgot to mention that today is a holiday."

Becca snorted, and their grandmother pointed a finger toward both of them. "All right, you two. Don't get smart." Then she tilted her head toward the Sweet Stop and squinted at the folks already lining up in front of the place to view the parade. "Boy, I'm glad we already put our blankets out. It's really getting crowded. But I don't see Haley over there yet. Hey, wait a minute. Isn't that the writer coming out of the candy store?"

Troy followed his grandmother's gaze and immediately spotted Destiny Porter, her chocolate hair shining beneath the lights covering the Sweet Stop's awning. It flowed freely tonight, not contained by a ponytail the way it'd been the past two times he saw her, and her attire was different, too, a casual T-shirt, shorts and sandals. She looked very…pretty. He swallowed. "Yes, that's her."

"Oh, I'm glad she's here," Becca said. "Mama told me about meeting her at church last night. I guess I missed seeing her when I went to pick Lily up from class."

"Well, you should meet her," Troy's grandmother said, already heading toward the candy shop. "We want her to get to know the family well so she'll consider putting us in her book. I should show her where A Likely Story is, too, so she can talk to David Presley about having a book signing sometime." She gasped. "Oh, my, look at the size of that ice-cream cone she's carrying."

"I want ice cream!" Lily yelled.

"I'll get you some." Troy noticed the tower of ice-cream scoops balancing atop Destiny's sugar cone at the same time he heard the high school band start up and knew the parade was about to begin. A little boy, obviously excited, shoved past Destiny when he heard the band and sent the top scoop plunking to the ground. Frowning, she leaned down to pick up the round blob, and another scoop joined the first on the sidewalk. Her lip trembled.

"Hey, the parade is starting!" his grandmother said. "Let's get to our spot. Becca, yell at the boys to stop playing football and come on over before the band blocks their path. Troy, ask the writer if she wants to come sit with us." She was so busy barking orders that she didn't notice Destiny's dilemma, but Troy did, and so did his sister.

"Oh, Troy, will you go help her?" Becca's voice was tender.

"Sure." He'd already started that way.

"I want ice cream," Lily repeated. "Please?"

"Here, I'll take her," Becca said, but Troy shook his head.

"Nah, it may help to have her along." His niece had a way of making everyone smile, and he didn't think it'd hurt to bring her, since Destiny was obviously having a hard time.

"Ah, gotcha, good idea." Becca must've followed his reasoning and nodded her approval.

Troy gently lifted Lily off his shoulders and put her by his side. "Lily, we're going to go help that lady who dropped her ice cream, okay?"

"Okay. And then we'll get me some, too, right?"

"Right."

Becca pulled her cell phone from her pocket and read the display. "Oh, Joey has been assigned to start the parade, so he'll be in the police car in front of the band."

"Daddy's in the parade?"

"He sure is. So, Troy, bring Lily on over after you

get her ice cream, and we can wave at Joey together. I'll go tell our brothers to stop the football game before they take out one of the band members." She jogged over to the grassy area where the guys were still playing while Troy headed toward the woman having a difficult time picking up cold ice cream from the warm pavement...and piercing his heart with her tears.

Chapter Four

Destiny didn't know what she'd been thinking to get the triple scoop of rocky road then try to maneuver through this crowd. She'd planned to sit in the candy shop to eat the treat, but every table had been filled. And then, coming outside, she realized the sidewalk was even more congested than before she'd entered the store. Now she had two blobs of ice cream melting rapidly, and she sure didn't want any of these sandal-clad kids stepping in her mess. No reason for someone else's day to be ruined because she'd tried to drown her sorrows in ice cream.

But the stuff was melting fast, and the people were crowding her, and she couldn't figure out how to pick it up and get it to a trash can before it slid through her fingers. Each time she bent over, someone bumped her, and then more ice cream fell out of the cone.

"Why do you have to make everything so difficult?" Her mother's words, spoken numerous times throughout Destiny's life, echoed through her head, and tears slipped free. She'd thought the ice cream would help her feel better, but she *had* made every-

thing more difficult, getting the monster-size cone instead of something normal, and now she was paying the price. Her mother, if she were here, would happily say she told her so.

Destiny thought of how she'd made the success of her magazine more difficult, too, when she promised the advertisers—and her subscribers—that she'd publish the "True Southern Gentleman's Love Letters." What if she couldn't befriend Troy Lee soon enough? What if she couldn't find enough ways to run into the guy and convince him to give her the rights to run those amazing stories of his heart?

His letters were private, hence the reason Destiny felt so guilty every time she read them. But she kept reading them, absorbing them, dreaming about them. Or rather, dreaming about a guy like Troy. What would he do if he knew she'd read his secret desires for his bride? And what would he do when she told him she wanted the rest of the world to read them, too?

"Here, let me help."

Destiny recognized the calm, deep voice, which stood out over the cheering crowd. Sure enough, she looked up to see the very guy she'd been dreaming about scooping up the remainder of her cold mess with a couple of napkins, then tossing it in a nearby can. "Might as well throw the whole thing away, don't you think?" He reached for the cream-covered cone and Destiny let him take it, his large fingers easing her smaller ones away as he took what was left and also pitched it in the can.

"Uncle Troy said we can get you another one, since you dropped yours." A little blue-eyed girl had her face so close to Destiny's that their noses nearly touched. "We got the napkins from the hot-dog cart so we could help you. Are you sad you dropped your ice cream? 'Cause we can get you some more. And I'm gonna get some, too, right, Uncle Troy?"

"That's right." He tilted his head toward the little girl holding tight to his other hand. "This is Lily, by the way, my niece."

"I'm sorry you're so sad," Lily said. "I get sad sometimes, and ice cream makes me feel better."

"That was what I was going for," Destiny admitted, a smile tugging at her lips thanks to the adorable little girl.

"But we gotta hurry, 'cause Daddy is in the parade, and I don't want to miss him, but I need my ice cream, too." She yanked at Troy's hand. "Come on, Uncle Troy. The band is getting louder."

"She's right. We'd better get y'all some ice cream quick." He led the way back into the ice-cream shop, which had cleared out tremendously with the sounds of the parade starting. "Hey, Jasmine, Lily needs a single scoop of chocolate in a cake cone. And Destiny needs a…" He looked to Destiny, but the pretty blonde teen behind the counter interrupted.

"Did you eat all of that rocky road already?"

Destiny grabbed a couple of wet wipes from a dispenser near the display case and cleaned the goo off her fingers. "Nah, the sidewalk wanted it more than I did."

"She dropped it," Lily explained. "But Uncle Troy's getting her another one. Do you want a real big one again?"

"No." Destiny shook her head. "Definitely not. Just a single scoop of rocky road this time, in a sugar cone, please."

"Okay." The teen began serving up the order. "How about you, Troy? You want one, too?"

"Yeah, the usual."

She nodded. "Single scoop vanilla in a sugar cone, coming up."

Destiny couldn't hold back her look of surprise, and he grinned. "Guess I'm not as ambitious as you when it comes to ice cream."

"Actually, I was thinking you're the smart one. Vanilla wouldn't make as much of a mess, and the triple scoop isn't all it's cracked up to be."

"Unless you're counting cracks on the sidewalk," he said, and Destiny laughed.

Jasmine put the three cones in a white plastic holder on the counter, took Troy's money and shook her head. "Pitiful joke, Troy."

"Thanks." He picked up his ice cream and then handed Lily hers.

Destiny got her cone. "I didn't mean for you to pay for mine."

"Didn't ask if you meant for me to or not. I did what I wanted to do."

One dark brow lifted, along with one corner of his mouth. The look reminded Destiny of a little boy who knew he was cute and expected an adult to acknowledge the fact. Seeing it on a boy made Destiny grin; seeing it on Troy made her fight a swoon.

"But you can thank me if you like."

Did he have any idea the effect he had on women?

Even the teen behind the counter gazed adoringly at Troy, who was completely clueless about the admiration being hurled his way. And Destiny felt her own sadness lift, merely from being around the guy. "All right, then. Thanks."

The other side of his mouth kicked up to match the first, and Destiny was treated to a full, and quite beautiful, smile. "You're welcome."

"Oh, the band is getting louder, and I hear Daddy's siren!"

"Well, come on, let's get you out there." He started toward the door, while Destiny hung back near the counter. The tables had cleared out now, with everyone heading to watch the parade. She could sit down and eat her ice cream in peace and without risking another spill. Troy had cleaned up her mess, bought her ice cream and made her feel better about life in general. She didn't expect him to include her in his nightly activities, too…unless, say, he really wanted to. Because she'd quickly figured out she liked being included in Troy's world—liked it very much, in fact.

"Don't worry, one scoop will be much easier to carry in the crowd. And you don't want to miss the parade. Bet you haven't seen anything like it in Atlanta." He held the door open and paused, with Lily pulling steadfastly at his arm. "You are coming with us, aren't you? Lily's kind of tired of waiting."

"Yes, I am, come on, Uncle Troy!"

"That okay with you, Lily?" Destiny asked. "For me to watch the parade with y'all?"

"Yes!" She took a big swipe at her chocolate ice

cream with her tongue. "But come on, we have to hurry!"

Destiny moved to catch up with them, then followed in Troy's wake as he wove through the crowd. It didn't take but a few seconds to see his destination, to a group yelling excitedly at the approaching police car. In the center, and screaming with the most enthusiasm, was his adorable grandmother. Watching the feisty lady, she could see how the woman wouldn't have thought twice about mailing some of her grandson's love letters in to the magazine's contest. Unfortunately, she also didn't think twice about the necessity of gaining his permission.

"We're glad you made it!" she screamed to Destiny. "You'll want to see the parade so you can put it in your book!" Then she turned toward the police car moving closer and waved her hands. "Hey, mister, throw me something!"

The policeman shook his head but his smile grew wide, and he indeed tossed her an abundance of assorted candies.

"Look what your daddy threw us, Lily!" she called. "Come here, Greatie will help you grab them up!" Then she dropped to the ground with all of the kids and scooped the goods into a homemade tote.

Destiny was so taken with the scene that she almost forgot about her ice cream.

"Better eat that quick." Troy pointed to the melting treat. "Because I have it under good authority the majority of the cars and floats are tossing candy, and you'll want to get some." He'd already killed off his cone before the police car passed, but she still had half of her scoop and the entire cone left. "And some of those kids get kind of crazy with the candy tossing. They've been known to pelt a few faces, accidentally of course. Wouldn't want you to lose an eye to a rogue Jolly Rancher."

She laughed. "No, I wouldn't want that either." Then she picked up her pace eating the cone.

"That was my daddy!" Lily squealed. "Did you see him?"

The question was obviously directed to Destiny, and she took another lick of her ice cream and then nodded. "I sure did."

"Isn't he great?" A ring of chocolate surrounding her lips emphasized the little girl's broad smile.

"Yes," Destiny said, enjoying all of this more than anything she'd experienced in a long time, "he is."

"Here, take one of these." Troy's grandmother handed her a crimson tote similar to the one she used to gather candy. "It'll help you get more loot."

Destiny examined the bag and now noticed it had "Aidan's Grandma" appliquéd in gray on the side. A closer look showed that each bag identified a different name, with the one Destiny held emblazoned with "Troy's Grandma." Glancing up at the dark-haired man at her side, she saw Troy laugh.

"She's fairly proud of her grandchildren. She's made one of those for each of us, and she uses them for everything from parade loot to grocery shopping," he said. "You'll definitely catch enough candy to fill that one up."

And when she turned, another waterfall of bubble gum and jawbreakers headed her way from the top of the football team's flatbed truck. The players seemed to have more fun trying to peg members of the audience than riding in the parade. In fact, they made it look like a sport.

Destiny gathered another batch of candy and dropped it in Lily's bag. The little girl laughed, thanked her and then continued picking up candy from the ground with her mom and great-grandma. When Destiny stood to see the next float, a large Ring Pop nearly pegged her between the eyes. Thankfully, Troy saw it coming and snagged it with one hand.

"Hey, watch it," he warned the bulky football player on the back of the flatbed.

"Sorry, Troy, didn't realize how much I put on the toss." He shrugged, then yelled to Destiny, "Sorry, ma'am!"

"It's okay!" she yelled back, as the truck moved farther away and a group of young cloggers stopped in front of them to dance.

By the time the parade ended, Destiny's bag bulged with candy. She stepped toward Troy's grandma and held up the heavy tote. "I need to give your bag back."

"Oh, I want the bag back, but I got plenty of candy on my own. Just give it to me another time. You still coming out to see our fishing hole on Saturday?"

Destiny nodded. "I am."

"Then you can bring it to me then. No worries. But keep the candy. Lily and I got plenty for ourselves, didn't we, sweetie?"

The little girl yanked a red lollipop out of her mouth, causing her to emit a loud smack. "We sure did."

"Lily, why don't we walk over to the other side of

the square and see if we can find Daddy before he has to go back to work?" A pretty dark-haired woman who Destiny had already determined must be Troy's sister stepped toward them, the tote dangling from her arm identifying "Rebecca's Grandma." She looked about the same age as Destiny. "Hey," she said. "I'm Troy's sister, Becca, and Lily's mom. It's nice to meet you."

"Oh, sorry," Troy said. "Becca, this is Destiny. Destiny, this is Becca."

"Nice to meet you."

Lily's mouth smacked with another removal of her lollipop. "I'm ready to go see Daddy."

"I'll go with y'all," Jolaine Bowers said, then she scanned the crowd. "Aidan went over to the sporting goods store to help James lock up. I'm not sure where the young boys headed off to, probably talking to some of the high school girls. What about you, Troy? Want to come with us, or are you sticking around here?" Her eyes glanced to Destiny, but she didn't look as though she disapproved. Then again, she probably thought Troy was helping their family business make its way into Destiny's nonexistent novel. She had no idea Destiny wanted to put Troy's words into print.

"Gonna stay here for a while," he said.

Jolaine, Becca and Lily all waved goodbye before they darted across the center of the square with a large portion of the crowd. Troy stood his ground, while Destiny felt a little awkward about what to do now.

"You want some candy?" She held the bag open for him to peek inside.

"Nah, I ate my quota while the parade passed." He looked down at her as he spoke and reminded Destiny of the difference in her five foot five and his six foot plus. Something about standing next to the guy made her feel very small, and very protected. She'd never liked feeling dependent on a guy, but she liked the way *this* felt, whatever it was.

He nodded toward a hot-dog cart at the street corner. "Come over here for a minute. I need to get something for you."

"Oh, I'm not hungry. At all." She hadn't stopped eating since she'd arrived at the square, and even though the entire consumption involved sugar, she still couldn't add anything else to the mix. Especially not a hot dog.

He laughed. "I'm not buying food. Just trust me." He took a step toward the silver metal cart, and Destiny followed. Oddly enough, she did trust him, and trust was something she had a hard time with, especially when it involved guys.

But she trusted Troy.

Would he ever trust her? Enough to say yes when she asked about those letters?

They neared the hot-dog stand and Troy lifted a finger toward the older man handing out the food. "Hey, Marvin, I need a few more napkins, please. And a cup of water, if you don't mind."

"Sure, Troy." The man lifted a roll of paper towels, pulled a couple off and then filled a cup with water from a pitcher. After wrapping the napkins around the cup, he handed it to Troy. "Want a hot dog or two, as well? I've marked them down to half price since the parade ended."

"Not this time. I'm afraid we filled up on candy."

"Happens to the best of us," the older man said with a grin. Then he turned his attention to a family making their way toward the cart and eyeing the remaining hot dogs in the warmer. "Hang on. Customers."

"No problem." Troy stepped away from the cart and indicated for Destiny to come along. He stopped beside a bench, then reached for her tote. "Let me put this down for a minute while I help you out."

"Help me out?" Destiny watched as he placed the bag on the wooden bench, then put a finger beneath her chin and gently tilted her head. She felt her pulse race, everything tingling from the place where his warm finger touched her skin. She blinked, swallowed and wondered if she was about to experience a kiss from the guy currently making her head spin with his gentle touch.

He smiled, removed his finger and unwrapped the napkins from the cup. Then he dipped them in the water, lifted them back out and instructed, "Close your eyes."

This was the most bizarre thing any guy had ever done, but she followed his command and slid her eyes shut. What did he plan to do with those napkins? And did it involve kissing? Because right now, she very much wanted to be kissed.

The cool paper touched the tender skin beneath her right eye, and she gasped, then opened her eyes to see Troy's face merely inches from hers.

"I'm not sure what upset you earlier, but I'd like to wipe away the evidence, if that's okay with you." He gently guided the wet napkins along her skin.

Realization dawned. "Oh, dear, I have mascara streaks?"

His smile was soft. "Just a few. And it's okay. I understand that sometimes girls need a good cry. I grew up with a sister, you know. You okay now? You seemed to enjoy the parade."

Her throat thickened at his compassionate tone, as though he honestly cared whether she'd been upset. "I am okay now, thanks."

He dipped the napkins again, let the excess water drip free and then cleaned beneath her other eye while Destiny felt her control slip. She could see how girls would fall in love with Troy's letters. She could see how girls could fall in love with Troy, period.

He moved a finger beneath her chin again and examined her face as he slowly removed the tearstains. And for the briefest moment, Destiny felt it again, that inclination that Troy was thinking about easing closer, touching his lips to hers and letting her learn how incredible it would be to experience his kiss.

"Okay, customers are gone now. So, who's your friend there? Don't believe we've met." The man from the hot-dog cart clapped his hands together as Troy finished up.

"There," he said quietly while the older man stepped toward them, "good as new."

Destiny swallowed, forcing her heartbeat to slow and her breathing to return to normal. "Thanks."

The older man stepped between them and faced Destiny. "You're a pretty girl, young lady."

She smiled at the sweet man, even if he may have ruined a first kiss. "Thank you."

"I'm sorry, I forgot the introductions again. Marvin, this is Destiny. She's visiting Claremont to write stories about living in a small town. Destiny, this is Marvin Tolleson. He runs Nelson's Variety Store." Troy pointed to one of the shops across the square. "They've got the best hamburgers and milkshakes you'll ever taste."

"And hot dogs," Marvin added. "You'll have to try one sometime, when you aren't too full from sweets."

"I'll do that."

"And if you're writing about Claremont, I've got plenty of stories to share. Been here since I was born, you know. Seventy-four years and counting. Me and my sweet Mae got married right there in front of that fountain in the middle of the square back in 1958."

Destiny sensed a love story that needed to be written. "I'd like to hear about how you met, what tips you'd give young couples starting out and how you feel your marriage benefited from living in a small town." She smiled. "That's exactly the type of thing I write about, in fact."

His wrinkled cheeks slipped high with his grin. "Well, we're over at the variety store every day, open at seven and don't close till the last customer's served. Though we both take a nap or two in between. We live above the store, so even if we're taking a power nap, we aren't far away. You'll be able to find us."

Destiny laughed. "If you're napping, I'll come back when you're awake."

"Sounds like a plan." He glanced at the thinning crowd. "Looks like folks are heading home. I'm gonna pack up the cart until tomorrow night's First Friday

Festival. You'll want to see that, too, if you're writing about small-town living. First Friday is the best part of a new month, if you ask me. Definitely worth writing about."

"Then I won't miss it."

"Good deal." He began tucking napkins, buns and paper plates into the appropriate slots on his cart.

"You want me to help you roll that over to your store?" Troy asked.

The man closed the silver lid and winked. "Help me? I figured you'd do the job."

Troy laughed and moved to the end of the cart. "You want to walk with us over to Nelson's?" he asked Destiny.

"Sure she does." Marvin tweaked Destiny's arm. "That way she'll get to meet Mae. You want to meet my sweetie, don't ya?"

"Of course." Destiny walked beside the man, the two of them following Troy as he pushed the cart along the sidewalk and toward the variety store. They passed several people along the way, and each time, Marvin and Troy addressed them by name, and then one or the other would perform a quick introduction of Destiny. It amazed her how friendly the townspeople were and how they seemed genuinely interested in meeting the newcomer. Back home in Atlanta, people were friendly with traditional Southern home hospitality, but a smile or a simple "hello" did the trick. Here there was something different to the greetings. It reminded her of Christmas, when everyone is happy and excited and pleased with life.

Christmas in July. Was Claremont always like this?

"There she is." Marvin's tender tone emphasized the love he still had for the woman he'd married over fifty years ago, and Destiny felt her heart clench. What would it be like to find that kind of lasting love?

Mae Tolleson had silver hair that framed a round face. She wore a checked blue dress with a white apron and stood at the doorway to their store distributing hugs to the customers as they left for the evening. Looking up, she spotted her husband. "Marvin, how'd the cart do?"

"Ah, the cart did okay, but I was amazing." He chuckled as he neared his wife, and she rewarded him with a hug and a kiss on both cheeks.

"And modest," she said, peeking over his shoulder when he hugged her tighter. "I haven't met you before, have I?"

Marvin broke the hug and flicked a thumb toward Destiny. "Mae, this is Destiny. She's a writer visiting Claremont to tell the world about small-town living. And she's interested in writing about us."

"About us?"

"How you met, fell in love, married and stayed together," Destiny explained. "It's rare nowadays to see a couple stay together and even rarer to see them still in love after so many years. I think my readers would enjoy hearing your story."

"Why, that's so sweet," Mae said, the last word stretching with her yawn. "Oh, excuse me."

"Kind of past our bedtime," Marvin said. "But you don't need to talk to us right now, do you? You could come back tomorrow if you want, and we can share our story. Will that work?"

"That'd be great."

"Come at lunchtime, and we'll feed you real good," he added.

"He's telling the truth," Troy said. "Nelson's makes the best lunch around. I'd recommend the cheeseburger."

"That's Troy's favorite," Mae said, and then she looked from Troy to Destiny. "Are you two…friends?"

"We just met this week, but Troy has offered to help me with my writing, show me the ins and outs of small-town living."

A look passed from Mae to Marvin, and Destiny could tell they'd gotten the wrong idea about her relationship with the handsome mechanic. But she couldn't come up with a single thing to say that would dispel their thoughts, especially since she was still resisting the crazy urge to kiss him. So she remained quiet, and when the duo bid them good-night and headed inside to lock up their store, she wondered what it'd be like to have a guy like Troy look at her the way Marvin looked at Mae.

Chapter Five

Today I decided I want six kids. Granted, I know you'll have a say in this as well, but I thought I'd let you know while I have it on my mind. See, I just got back from Claremont Hospital. The whole family went last night and waited the ten hours that Becca was in labor. She was amazing. There's no other way to explain it. The nurse let the family go back to see her throughout the night, and I was in there twice when big contractions hit. She grabbed my hand and gritted her teeth while thick tears streamed down her cheeks, and I found myself crying, too. Joey didn't like seeing her in pain; neither did I. I know I won't like seeing you in pain either. But then, this morning, Lillian Grace entered the world, and Becca's pain became the most exquisite joy I've ever witnessed.

Okay, about the six kids. If you don't want that many, I'm open to whatever you want. It's just that, well, I love my big family and the wonderful craziness that occurs when we're all truly a part of each other's worlds, spiritually, emotionally and physically. It's the way God meant things to be, I believe. Families caring about each other, caring for each other. I can't wait to see what you think of the people who are so near and dear to my heart. I know they will love you. I also hope and pray that your family will feel the same about me.

Oh, Joey and Becca have decided to call their little girl Lily. She has a head full of black hair and bright blue eyes. I personally think she's the prettiest baby I've ever seen, but I can already tell I'm going to be a bit prejudiced toward my new niece. May spoil her a bit, too, but hey, that's all part of the fun, right? Looking forward to you meeting her.

Love in advance…and then forever,

Troy

Destiny had pictured the black-haired, blue-eyed baby when she first read this particular letter, but now that she'd met Lily in person, she could see why Troy was so smitten. The little girl was beautiful and undeniably adored her uncle Troy.

And now that Destiny had met his family, and personally viewed the closeness they shared and the delight they got in simply being together, she understood why he also wanted a large family. She had never wanted to have more than one or two children before, but now she found herself considering the possibility of a houseful. Six kids, four girls and two boys, all of them with jet-black hair and Caribbean-blue eyes.

Then she blinked. Those were Troy's children. And for some reason, she'd put them in *her* house.

Sitting in her favorite rocker on the front porch of the B and B, she fanned herself with Troy's letter about baby Lily and tried to get a grip on this attraction that escalated each time she read one of his letters, or each time she saw him, or each time she thought of him. Even today's blog, where she wrote about meeting the country boy with the big heart, made her sound like a swooning teen. But even though she'd deleted the thing and rewritten it twice, each time the message came across the same, and she'd finally gotten tired of trying to hide her fascination and hit the post button.

After writing the blog and then spending an abundance of time scanning all of her sister's engagement photos on Facebook, she'd gone to Nelson's Variety Store for lunch. The cheeseburger was indeed amazing, as Troy had promised, as was Marvin and Mae's love story. She planned to post it to the site tomorrow. But even as she'd listened to the two tell about the first time they saw each other, how Mae had been too shy to acknowledge Marvin's request to walk her home from school and how they'd finally admitted their love and then, within two weeks, pledged their wedding vows at the old Claremont courthouse…Destiny found herself wondering what it'd be like to spend fifty-plus years with a man.

No, not with any man. With Troy Lee.

"I need help." She lifted the cool glass filled with Annette Tingle's lemonade, today's garnished with frozen strawberries, and sipped the drink.

"Anything I can do?"

Startled, Destiny coughed on the lemonade but managed to keep it in her mouth until she swallowed. The tart liquid burned as it headed down the wrong way, and her eyes watered while she concentrated on taking another sip to clear her throat. "I didn't hear you come out," she finally said to Mr. Tingle.

"I'm sorry I startled you. I'd have yanked on your arm or something, but I've always heard you don't touch a person as long as they're coughing." He leaned against the white banister with concern clearly etched across his face.

She swiped at her tears and grinned. "I've always heard the same thing, and it's okay. I was just thinking about something else and wasn't paying attention."

"That's because I walked around the house. Took the trash out for Annette and thought I'd check the porch to make sure all of the decorations were holding up for First Friday. Didn't mean to eavesdrop, but I will try to help, if there's anything I can do. And were you thinking about some*thing* else, or some*one* else?"

Destiny glanced at the letter still in her hand.

"That's what I thought," he said, eyeing the folded paper. "That a love letter?"

"No," she said, then realized that wasn't true. "I mean yes, it is, but it isn't to me."

His brows dipped, mouth slid to the side. "O-kay. And I'm guessing that's the problem?"

Destiny sighed. "Not really." And then she realized that also wasn't exactly true. "Yeah, maybe." Because she felt a strong surge of jealousy toward the woman for whom these letters were intended. Jealousy toward any woman who held Troy's attention. And that was a problem. A big one. They weren't even friends yet; if they were, she'd have no trouble asking him if she could run his love letters. In his mind, she was simply visiting from Atlanta to write about small-town living.

But last night, when he'd wiped her tearstains away, she'd felt *something*.

Had she imagined it because she wanted him to feel something, too? Or had he actually thought about kissing her?

"Well, I'm going to pray that everything works out the way you want it to." L.E.'s statement brought her thoughts back to the here and now, on the porch, instead of to last night's maybe-near-kiss.

"You're going to pray for me?" Her heart clenched because she suspected the man wasn't merely saying words; he'd really pray for her. She'd never had anyone say they'd pray for her before, and she wasn't certain anyone had ever prayed for her before, period.

"Sure." He grinned. "And I'll pray that the next love letter you read *will* be intended for you."

"Thank you." She had no doubt the next love letter she'd read would be another of Troy's, since she'd developed some kind of addiction to reading them repeatedly. And his grandmother wanted them returned, so she'd need to do that soon. But she wasn't ready to yet. It wouldn't hurt to wait another day…or two.

He settled more firmly against the porch rail and crossed his arms. "I wrote a few love letters to Annette, back in the day. She wrote some to me, too. I still have them, tucked in a keepsake box beneath our bed." He frowned. "Been years, though, since we exchanged love letters."

"Really? Why?" She knew the moment she asked that the question was probably too personal, but he didn't seem to get offended.

"You know, I'm not sure. I guess in the beginning you go about trying to make sure the person knows how you feel, so you write it all out and tell them. Then, as the years go on, I guess you assume they know."

She thought about the lucky lady who'd get the letters Troy had written, and how sad it'd be if the woman never received another. "Don't you think it'd still be good to tell the person?"

"Yes, yes, I do." He nodded. "Maybe I'll surprise Annette and write one again. If memory served, she made a bigger fuss over those letters than the most elaborate gifts that I've given her over the years. And I've gotta admit, I enjoyed receiving hers, too. There's something about words from the heart, isn't there?"

Her hand tightened around Troy's letter. "Yes, there is."

He took a step toward the house. "Don't know why I haven't thought of doing that again, writing to Annette that way." Then he winked at Destiny. "Thanks for reminding me."

"You're welcome." She made a mental note to learn the Tingles' love story before she left Claremont and, if they said it was okay, to share it with her readers.

Her phone rang, and L.E. held up a hand in a wave before heading into the house. Destiny glanced at the display then answered. "Hey, everything okay?"

Rita huffed out an exasperated breath. "Honestly,

you have got to start trusting my ability to keep things going."

Destiny grinned. "Sorry. Okay then, forget that. How's your day been?"

"Absolutely fabulous. Amazing, even." Rita's excitement pulsed through each syllable.

"Really? Something to do with *Southern Love?* Did we get more subscribers? Or advertisers?"

Rita answered, "Yes to all. Definitely something to do with *Southern Love*. Yes to more subscribers, though not as many as we need. And a few more advertisers, too!"

"Seriously? Any idea why?"

"You don't know? You haven't looked at today's blog?"

Destiny placed her glass on the table, then reached for the computer bag she'd propped against the next rocker. "Not since I posted it." She already had her laptop in hand and wasted no time booting it up. "What's going on?"

"Your post, that's what. Everyone is falling in love with Troy, and they still don't even know his name. Lots of folks are wondering exactly where you are, and they're trying to get clues from your post. Thankfully, lots of small towns in the South had parades last night for the Fourth. Everyone wants to meet the guy who cleaned up your ice cream, spent his evening catering to a three-year-old princess and his crazy family and then also managed to give you goose bumps when he wiped your tears. I mean, it's every girl's dream. Or rather, he is every girl's dream." She laughed. "You should see how many posts are offering to pay you for his number."

Destiny had the page up and saw those comments firsthand, all three-hundred-plus of them. "We haven't had this many responses since we started the blog."

"I know, and the advertisers have noticed, too. Our site hits have tripled today, with lots of folks already subscribing to the next issue of the magazine because they want to read Troy's love letters! Isn't that great?"

"Yeah, great." But Rita's excitement wasn't transferring to Destiny, not at all. Because she still hadn't gotten a commitment from Troy that would allow her to run the letters, and now she wasn't all that certain she wanted to share them.

"Something wrong?"

Destiny blinked. Nothing should be wrong. She should be happy, ecstatic even. And one way or another, she was going to find the means to pull that off. "No, I'm just shocked. This is great. I'm glad you told me. Really." She picked up her tone a little, and Rita bought it.

"I know! I wish I could see your face right now."

Destiny nodded but didn't answer. She didn't want her friend to see her face because Rita would undoubtedly be able to tell that happiness wasn't anywhere in the equation.

"Okay, I'm going to start running these credit cards for all of the subscribers. Thankfully, the majority used PayPal, but I've got quite a few to go. This is awesome, huh?"

"It is. Hey, I've got to go." She continued scrolling through comment after comment of how drool-worthy the bighearted country boy seemed. "I'll call you back later."

Rita said bye and disconnected, while Destiny read as many as she could handle, then closed the window and shut down the computer.

"This is exactly what I wanted. I should be happy." She slid the computer in the bag, then reached for her lemonade and took a big sip. "I *will* be happy."

Her phone rang again. Assuming Rita had remembered more to tell her, she answered in her best "happy" voice, "Hey, forget something?"

"That's funny, I was going to ask you the same thing. Have you forgotten to call me since you high-tailed it to Alabama?"

Destiny took another sip of lemonade, held the chilled liquid in her mouth for a moment to hopefully cool her spirit, then swallowed. "Hi, Mom."

"That's it? I don't hear from you in days, and you haven't even called about your sister's engagement, and you say, 'Hi, Mom'?"

"I talked to Bevvie about the engagement and looked at the photos this morning. I'm really excited for her."

"I can tell."

"I am, Mom. So, how's everything there? How's Dad?"

"Still at the hospital, of course. He had a surgery this afternoon, and I suppose it ran late...again."

"I'm pretty sure the patients pay him by the procedure, not by the hour."

"I'm not starting with you tonight, Destiny. I sim-

ply want to know when you're planning to come back
to Atlanta."

"As soon as I get what I need for the next issue."

"Honey, when are you going to realize that you
need to give up? You've given it a valiant effort, but it's
been, what, a year now? I know you're out of money,
and I don't understand why you don't let us help, or
why you don't try to get a job that really uses your
degree."

"My degree is in journalism, and I am using it,
Mom. And why do you think I'm out of money?" She
was close, but somehow she always got the bills paid,
and she wasn't ready to declare defeat yet. Plus, she
had new subscribers and advertisers today, thanks to
her blog post about Troy. She'd continue to post more
and hopefully share his letters with the world soon,
and everything would be just fine. She couldn't wait
to tell her mother all about it, when it happened.

"I've looked in your refrigerator, dear. No one lives
on bagels and orange juice. Of course, it does make it
easier to clean when it's empty, I suppose."

Destiny's skin bristled. Her mother judged how she
was doing by how well her fridge was filled? "One
person doesn't require a whole lot of food."

"And that's another thing. Are you even dating anyone now? What happened to that Beasley boy? Mike,
wasn't it? He was so nice and could have taken care
of you for life."

Destiny easily translated her mother's words. *He
was rich, and you'd have had it made, like me.* She
wanted to point out how happy "having it made" had
made her mom, but she didn't want to start a fight.

Really. "Mike got married in June." He'd also broken up with Destiny via a text message after he met his future bride at the beach.

Future bride. That's how Troy sometimes referred to his wife in his letters. Destiny unfolded the one she'd been reading and scanned his tender words again. Six kids with Troy. She shouldn't even dream about it, but for some reason, she couldn't stop at least considering the possibility.

"What is it about the guys you choose? Bevvie met Jared and said she knew he was the one. Haven't you felt that way about anyone?"

She glanced at the letter. Was *that* what was happening? And wouldn't that be her luck, that her heart would fall hook, line and sinker for a guy looking for someone totally different? Because Destiny wasn't the kind of "down home" girl he described in his letters. She didn't have the faith he listed as the most important quality for his future wife. And she certainly didn't know anything about being part of a big, happy family.

Her mother huffed out a breath. "You know, maybe if you actually did something with your life and got out in the real world a bit, you would meet someone and have a relationship, too."

Destiny swallowed past the urge to argue. It never did any good and would only make her feel worse. "Mom, I've got to go. There's a festival on the town square tonight."

After a pause, her mother snapped, "Working hard, I see."

"I'm writing stories about the people here, so going

to the town's activities is a part of my job. And yes, I *am* working hard." Though her current definition of working hard meant working hard to gain Troy's trust.

"Fine." Geneva cleared her throat. "Did you say you saw your sister's engagement photos?"

Destiny welcomed the subject change. "I did, and they were beautiful. Like I said, I'm very happy for them."

"They were beautiful, weren't they? I tried to capture the lighting right so that they practically glowed in the pictures, or that's the way I thought they turned out. What did you think?"

"That's how they looked, very pretty."

"I thought so, too." She sighed. "Destiny, think about coming home and letting us try to help you get a regular job. Your daddy and I have a lot of contacts, you know."

"I know." But she didn't want to work for any of their country-club friends. She wanted to go for her dream, and her dream was the magazine. She wished her mother understood.

"All right, then. Have fun at the festival."

Destiny blinked. What had happened in the past two minutes that changed her mother's tone and made her sound more like…a mother? "O-kay, I will."

"I do love you, you know."

"I love you, too." And as she disconnected, she realized that the words were true. She loved her mother, felt sorry for her sometimes, even. Because while she did have her tennis buddies and a few friends who were closer than others, the majority of the time she roamed that huge house by herself, watching the clock and waiting for her husband to return home. She usually seemed absolutely miserable, but every now and then, Destiny would hear a hint of happiness again. She'd thought she caught that a moment ago. Probably because of Bevvie's engagement. Yeah, that had to be it. Maybe if Destiny ever found "the one," her mother would find a little happiness for her, too.

Not wanting to spend any more time analyzing her mother's bizarre behavior, she decided to head to the First Friday Festival. Troy was undoubtedly on his date with Haley Calhoun, and so she planned to keep herself busy, very busy, so she wouldn't have time to wonder whether he had traded in his player reputation and decided that the pretty vet was "the one."

Destiny also didn't want to spend any time analyzing why that possibility hurt so much.

Troy typically wasn't nervous about dates, but that changed today. He wanted to do this right, treat Haley to an evening that would leave a great first-date impression and lead to a second date. But his plans were hindered by the realization that he actually wanted a second date this time. He was tired of his "player" status and ready to settle down. And he honestly felt God had put it on his heart this week to give a relationship more time, let it develop and see if God was giving him the opportunity to finally meet the woman he'd been writing to all of these years.

But today, when he should have been thinking about his date with Haley, he found himself remembering last night, about the way Destiny had joined in with his energized family to gather parade loot, the way her cheeks had flushed when he took her melted cone and their hands touched, and about the surge of emotion that overpowered him when he wiped her tearstains away.

He'd wanted to kiss her; he nearly had, in fact. And today, at lunch, he'd fought the urge to drive to Nelson's for a cheeseburger. No doubt he wouldn't have been going for the meal; he'd have been going for a chance to see the pretty writer.

But tonight, when he picked up Haley for their date, he'd promised himself to keep his mind focused on the here and now instead of on whatever had occurred between him and Destiny last night. Yet through dinner, even his small talk with Haley had been a little stilted. He'd taken her to Messina's, a charming Italian restaurant about ten minutes out from town and clearly the nicest place to eat around Claremont. The food had been terrific. But he hadn't felt the closeness he'd hoped for, and he suspected it was because he kept wondering what Destiny Porter was doing this evening.

Maybe he *was* a player.

"And then Dr. Graham brought his little girl Autumn in with a baby dove that had fallen out of the nest. The little girl was so concerned for the bird. It was precious." Haley chatted as they drove away from the restaurant. She'd talked about her job and her faith the majority of the date so far, and Troy could tell how much she loved her work. He admired it, in fact. She was obviously the kind of caring, compassionate woman he'd always wanted, so it didn't make sense that he wasn't hanging on to every word.

I should be feeling something here, Lord. Help me out. She seems perfect. Beautiful, intelligent, caring, and she's talked about You and her love of You. This is what I prayed for, the type of person I've been writing to.

"I love it when a child tries to help like that, don't you?" Her green eyes were alive with excitement. "We're going to be able to save that little bird because of Autumn and her sweet heart. Isn't that wonderful?"

"Yes, it is." He glanced at her. With the passenger window halfway down, her hair blew gently around her face and her happiness about the saved bird made her look even prettier. Beautiful, in fact. She had a look that stood out, silky white-blond hair, almond-shaped green eyes and a heart-shaped mouth. She was petite, probably five-two, a few inches shorter than Destiny.

Now where had *that* come from?

Haley rested her arm on the back of the seat and smiled. "What's on your mind?"

You. And Destiny. And the fact that if I keep this up, I'm earning my player credentials.

He cleared his throat and thought about what he'd planned for them to do next. "I thought we could either go to Hydrangea Park and see the botanical gardens or we could go to the First Friday Festival on the square. Your choice."

"I've heard about how they light up the gardens at the park at night, so I know I want to see them sometime, but Dr. Sheridan has been talking all week about how wonderful First Friday is, and I'd really like to do that, if it's okay with you."

That'd been his preference, too. They could visit the park anytime, but First Friday only occurred once a month, and Troy rarely missed the event. "First Friday it is. I think you'll enjoy it, especially since the square will still be decorated from the parade last night." His mind flashed to catching that piece of candy merely inches from Destiny's face. He shook the image away. "So you'll also get a chance to see everything they did for the holiday."

"I hate that I missed the parade. I got to updating this week's appointments on the computer, and then I noticed the receipts hadn't been posted, and then I heard one of the boarded dogs whining and decided to take him for a walk. Then the next thing I knew, I was walking all of them." She shrugged. "I tend to lose track of time when I'm working."

"Probably a good sign that you love your job." And that she was hardworking and committed. Two qualities Troy had always admired and had even written about a time or two in his letters.

"I do love it. Oh, dear, I haven't checked my phone in a while." She withdrew her cell from her purse and glanced at the display. "Dr. Sheridan is taking his family to First Friday tonight so I volunteered to handle any emergencies. The phone at the office is forwarded to my cell."

Troy nodded but wondered whether she'd considered their date when she volunteered to handle all emergencies.

"No messages, so we're good." She smiled, and Troy returned the gesture.

He was being too critical, and he'd stop that now.

That'd been part of the reason he hadn't had many repeat dates before; he wasn't going to let it ruin his interpretation of tonight. So she'd volunteered to take calls during their date; that wasn't necessarily a bad thing.

"Are all of those cars for the festival?"

He looked ahead to see vehicles lining both sides of the street, then pulled his truck in at the end. "Yeah, most everyone in town comes, as well as the majority of folks from the surrounding counties." He cut off the ignition. "Any kind of a festival is a pretty big deal around here, but First Fridays do tend to be the favorites, especially this one, since it follows the Fourth and will have all of the extra decorations."

Climbing out, he started around the truck with the intention of opening her door, but by the time he circled the front, she was already out, her hand shielding her eyes from the setting sun as she peered down the sidewalk toward the square.

"This looks incredible."

"It is." He held out a hand, trying to be a gentleman in spite of the fact that she seemed content in her independence, and he liked the way she slid her palm into his.

"Where do we start?" she asked.

"The back of Gina Brown's Art Gallery is up ahead, where all of those lights are hanging from the trees. She has a courtyard that leads inside, and usually she has artists set up painting there for First Friday."

"That sounds wonderful."

They walked hand in hand to the courtyard where several artists were indeed painting. Paper lanterns and tiny white lights dotted the huge magnolias that created a canopy over the courtyard. Gina noticed Troy and gracefully maneuvered past a couple of easels to greet them. "Troy, it's wonderful to see you again."

"Good to see you, too." He nodded toward Haley. "This is Haley Calhoun. She's the new vet, working with Dr. Sheridan."

"I believe I met you at church last Sunday morning, didn't I?" Gina asked.

"Yes, you did, but I didn't realize you are an artist. I'm looking forward to seeing your work."

Gina smiled. "My pieces are inside, but take a little time to view the art out here first. We have a lot of talent locally, and all of these artists will be offering the paintings from tonight in a wet paint sale."

"That sounds great," Haley said, still admiring the scene. "It's so beautiful out here."

"I'm glad you think so. I have some refreshments over by the rear entrance. Please help yourself. And we also have a children's area out front that you'll want to see. The kids are really enjoying themselves this evening with the face-painting artist. Oh, Troy, your family was out there the last time I went. Maybe they're still there."

"We'll check when we go out front, but even if we don't catch them here, I'm sure we'll see them before the night's over. They tend to stay at First Friday until everything closes."

"Thankfully, most folks do. And trust me, the shop owners love it." She looked to Haley. "This is great for local business, you know."

"I can see that." Haley released Troy's hand and moved closer to a young artist to get a better look at the giraffe he was painting.

Gina stepped nearer to Troy and whispered, "You make a beautiful couple, Troy. Striking enough to paint, I'd say."

He swallowed past the strange thickness in his throat. "Thanks." Then without any sort of explanation of their couple status, since he still didn't know how he'd explain it, he returned to his date, who was chatting with the artist about the realistic quality of his animal paintings.

"These would look amazing in the examination rooms at the animal hospital. I'm going to tell Dr. Sheridan about you. Can I have your card?"

Beaming at Haley, the guy handed her his card. Troy had no doubt he was not only taken by her enthusiasm for his work but also by her beauty. She was a pretty girl, striking, as Gina had said. And Troy should feel honored, thrilled even, that she was spending time with him tonight. He should have all of his focus on her, and he wished he could keep it there, instead of occasionally thinking about the pretty brunette he'd been with last night.

Haley tucked the card into her pocket, said goodbye to the smiling guy and looked back to Troy. "I'm loving this. Let's go inside and see what else she has."

They spent a few moments browsing Gina's personal paintings, the majority of them scenes from Claremont, and admiring her talent.

"We had a few galleries in Ocala but none that

showcased local artists. This is so unique, especially for a town the size of Claremont."

"We're really blessed to have so much to offer for a city of less than five thousand."

"I agree." She walked a little ahead of him as they moved toward the front of the store and the noise that emphasized the festival on the square. Laughter overpowered the profusion of sounds, with one giggle claiming dominion over the rest.

Troy recognized Lily's laugh immediately. "I think my family is still out front," he said as they walked through the doorway and, sure enough, found the majority of them on the sidewalk in the area Gina had termed the Children's Paint Zone.

"Uncle Troy!" Lily scrambled off a chair and ran toward him, then planted her feet and turned her face. "Do you like my butterfly?" Purple, pink and white glitter covered her right cheek in one of the most elaborate face-painting decorations he'd ever seen.

"It's beautiful, Lily." He picked her up and squeezed her while she emitted more giggles.

"Hey, are you Uncle Troy's friend, too?" She peered over his shoulder at Haley.

Haley laughed. "Yes, I am."

Lily wiggled in Troy's arms, and he put her on the ground so she could get closer to Haley. "Okay. You want to get a butterfly, too, or do you want something different? Miss Destiny got a butterfly like mine, but you can get something else if you want to."

Troy caught the reference and looked around to spot the woman he'd been thinking of throughout the day. "Miss Destiny got one?"

Lily nodded enthusiastically. "Yeah. She saw me at the toy store and helped me play with the dollhouses there, and then she came here to get her face painted, too, but then she went to talk to Miss Hannah, you know, my teacher from Sunday school." Her pigtails bobbed as she returned her attention to Haley. "You want to get a butterfly or something else? He does pretty horses, too, but I like the butterfly the best. What do you want?" She held out her tiny hand and smiled at Haley.

"A butterfly, definitely." Haley took Lily's hand and within seconds was perched in a chair next to a talented artist assigned to face painting. The look Haley gave Lily had "this child is so adorable" written all over it and it touched Troy's heart. But now he knew that Destiny had also spent time with Lily tonight, which meant she spent time with his family, too. He found himself wishing he could've seen the interaction. She'd enjoyed the parade so much, he knew that she probably enjoyed First Friday, also. But, scanning the crowd, he saw no sign of her.

"She went to talk to Hannah Graham." Becca's words were delivered softly, close to Troy's left ear. "You *are* looking for Destiny, aren't you?"

"Am I that obvious?"

"Only to me, but I've spent the entire twenty-five years of my existence around you, big brother. You can't hide what you're thinking from me." She nodded toward Haley, laughing as Lily explained to the painter exactly how she wanted the butterfly to look on her new friend's cheek. "Don't worry. I'm sure Haley didn't notice a thing."

Troy shook his head. "I don't know what's wrong with me. I'm with a great girl, one who from all appearances is everything I've been looking for—"

"The kind of girl you've been writing to, you mean," Becca interjected.

"Yeah. And yet I find myself continuing to think about one I barely know at all."

"Well, if you want to get right down to it…" Becca paused as their grandmother passed nearby. Both Becca and Troy knew she had eagle ears and would pick up this entire conversation if they didn't halt their progress. "Hey, Grandma, having fun?"

Jolaine Bowers nodded, winked at Haley and Lily, then wrapped her arms around Troy and Becca in a hug. "I sure am. I've been helping your grandfather at the sporting goods store, but Gina Brown sent word that she had plenty of snacks, so I'm getting us a bite to eat. Do you know where they're set up?"

"Out back in the courtyard," Troy said.

"Good deal. I'll be back in a jiff." She praised Lily's butterfly, then headed into the gallery.

"Now, what were you saying?" Troy asked his sister.

"That if you want to get right down to it, you don't know Haley Calhoun that well either, though I admit she seems wonderful."

"She's also living here now, and Destiny will be going back to Atlanta as soon as her writing is done. Wouldn't make sense to pursue a relationship with someone who's only here short-term."

"Yeah, well, love doesn't always make sense now, does it?"

Troy tried to keep his voice down, which probably wasn't necessary considering the noise from the crowd. "Love? Who said anything about love?"

She gave him her trademark smirk. "Uh-huh, nice try. You've finally decided you're ready for it, giving your heart, committing for life, the whole nine yards. I can tell."

"How's that?"

She shrugged. "You're acting different, and I think it's because you think you've found the right person."

"You know that this is my first date with Haley."

"And *you know* she isn't 'the one' I'm talking about. The whole time we've been standing here, you've been scanning the crowd, and you've hardly looked at the face-painting table, where your date is getting a beautiful butterfly on her cheek, courtesy of your niece's instructions." She let her smirk slide into a smile. "I'm right, aren't I? You're looking for Destiny."

"Yeah." He shook his head, baffled by his own emotions. "There's something about her. I don't know. It doesn't make any sense. I'm out with a great girl, and I've got another one on my mind." He looked around to make sure no one was eavesdropping, then said, "Did you know several of the women around town think I'm a player?"

Her laugh bubbled out. "Yes, I heard. Grandma told me, and then RuthEllen did as well, when she cut my hair yesterday. By the way, everyone in the beauty shop concurred."

"Super."

"And since you're out with one and thinking about another, you're wondering if they didn't peg you right with that label, aren't you?" Becca had always been able to read his thoughts; now, of course, was no exception.

"Yeah, maybe."

"Let me give you an example that might help you understand what you're feeling. Think back five years ago. I'd been dating Nolan Tucker for eight months when Joey pulled me over for speeding."

"And you talked your way out of a ticket."

She grinned. "Yeah, but that's not the important part. The important part is that I knew the moment I met him that I could love him for life. I ended everything with Nolan, and a week later, Joey and I had our first date."

"I recall you broke Nolan's heart back then."

"I couldn't help it. I was smitten from the first time I met Joey, and that's what I told Nolan. Anything else would have been lying to both of them…and to my heart."

He glanced at Haley. "If I remember right, Nolan left and took a job in another city."

She sighed. "He got a better job offer and he took it. I'm not completely positive I had anything to do with it. But in any case, that's not the point. I think you and I both know you've met the right one, and there isn't any reason in you stalling—or risking hurting another girl's heart—by not doing anything about it. And like you said, this is your first date with Haley. I doubt she'll pack up and move to another city if you tell her you've fallen for someone else."

"I haven't exactly fallen. I'm…interested. That's all I know, and I can't even pinpoint exactly why I can't stop thinking about her. But you realize that Destiny may not even return that interest." The truth of that hit his chest like a brick. "*She* may not be interested in *me*."

"Well, you'll never know until you ask, now, will you?"

A loud clearing of the throat caused both of them to turn and find their grandmother smacking lips covered in powdered sugar. She had a half-eaten fried apple pie clutched in one hand and two more balanced on a white paper plate in the other.

"Don't mind me. I'm just watching that beautiful Haley get a butterfly on her face." She winked at Troy, gave him a powdered-sugar kiss on the cheek and then continued toward the face-painting table. "Oh, Lily, you two look like twins now. Absolutely beautiful! This night is amazing, don't you think? Such wonderful things happen at First Friday." She looked back at Troy and smiled. "Wonderful things! Life-changing things. In fact, I'm going back to the store right now so I can tell your grandfather all about the great things happening tonight!" She turned and practically skipped down the sidewalk toward their sporting goods store.

"What got into her?" Troy asked.

"No idea." Becca took advantage of the short time they had before Haley's butterfly was complete to finish their conversation. "Listen, I knew when I met Joey that he was the one. I think you know pretty much the same thing right now, and it isn't about the girl you're with." She paused as though waiting for him to argue. Troy didn't bother; she was right. Then she nodded her head and continued, "So you need to think about that and don't miss the opportunity you have to spend time with Destiny while she's in town."

"And what about when she leaves?"

"Cross that bridge when it comes. If it is the real thing that you're feeling, it'll work out, and if you're smart, you'll ask God to help. He won't let you down." She snapped her fingers in front of his face. "And you can stop scanning the crowd. She went to the coffee shop with Hannah Graham to listen to Hannah's love story."

"Listen to her love story?"

"Yeah. Evidently Destiny got Marvin and Mae Tolleson to share the story of how they met, and then other people around town heard she was writing about how couples met and wanted to find out if they could be included in the paper, or article, or whatever." She grinned. "You see, the way you meet 'the one' is something special, and everyone likes to talk about it. So you should take note of *everything* that happens this week, just in case. Or, hey, you can probably put it all down in some of your letters. That's what you do best, after all."

"How does it look?" Haley stepped toward Troy with a red, white and blue glitter-embellished butterfly on her cheek. "Lily picked the colors to match all of the decorations."

"It looks great." He tried to sound enthusiastic, but now he had a new problem on his hands. How to gently end a relationship before it technically got started... and how to find out if the city girl was "the one."

No pressure.

Chapter Six

"So, are you going to see him today?" Rita asked.

"I'm on my way to his family's fishing hole right now. He works there on the weekends." Destiny passed another dirt road with no signage and prayed that the one she was supposed to take would have some form of identification. How did people find their way around down here?

"Their fishing hole." Rita's giggle echoed through the speaker on Destiny's phone. "That sounds so cool. Are you actually going to fish?"

"That's the plan. I told him that I've always wanted to, so he's going to teach me." She slowed down at the next dirt road, this one with an ancient mailbox at the end...with no name and no number. Her GPS said she still had a few miles to go, but even the GPS didn't display any identifiers for the obscure roads.

"Talk about going the extra mile to get him to let you publish those letters."

Destiny blinked. "Going the extra mile?"

"Pretending you want to learn how to fish and then doing it."

Rita's words were a punch to the chest. Obviously she didn't think a thing about insinuating Destiny had lied to Troy. Then again, why would she? That'd been a perfect way for both of them to get their way growing up, small fibs here and there to acquire whatever they wanted at the time. Back then it felt like a talent; now it felt pretty disgusting.

"I *have* always wanted to fish. I just never had an opportunity to learn."

"Really? I had no idea. You should've said something. My stepfather goes deep-sea fishing every spring and would've taken us along. And I'm sure we could've gotten some beach time, too. I never asked him about going because I didn't think I could stomach looking at a fish, much less touching one." She laughed. "Funny, I always assumed you felt the same way. Hard to picture you touching a fish. I bet your mother would die."

"This is a little different than deep-sea fishing, but for the record, I think I'd have enjoyed it." Destiny wondered how many other things she'd missed out on because people assumed she felt a certain way, presumably the same way as her mother who didn't like doing anything that might cause her to get dirty.

"That'll come in handy today, then, won't it? The fact that you actually *want* to know how to fish. Maybe fishing together, all of that outdoor bonding, will give you an opportunity to ask him about those letters. Because you need to get his permission to print them, and the sooner the better."

Outdoor bonding. The thought of that—with Troy—sounded very appealing. She was excited about spending time with him today, even if he went on a date with the pretty vet last night. Destiny had tried to keep her mind from wondering about the what-ifs of his first night out with Haley Calhoun. If they hit it off, then chances were that a relationship was officially getting started, and Destiny should feel good about that. Haley seemed to be the type of person that he'd written about in those amazing letters. Plus, she'd been at church Wednesday night, and she probably didn't come merely to see Troy, the way Destiny did. No, Haley was probably the real deal, faith-loving, Bible-toting and all of that. And from what Destiny could tell, she had a great personality, friendly and approachable. Last but not least, she was beautiful.

Destiny should be happy for Troy, potentially finding the woman he'd been writing to all of those years. But it was difficult to feel happiness when another green emotion kept pushing its way to the surface. *She* wanted to be on the receiving end of Troy's kind of affection. Destiny hadn't stopped thinking about how much she'd enjoyed her time with him at the parade. Or the fact that she'd kept hoping to see him on the square last night even though she'd known he was off somewhere having his date with Haley. Then she'd barely slept because she couldn't stop looking forward to seeing him today.

"Did you get a chance to read all of the emails we received before you started to the fishing hole?"

"Yes. Unreal, isn't it?"

"I'll say. They've been pouring in since you blogged that you'd met the country boy with the big heart. If he doesn't find 'the one' before we publish his letters,

I'm banking on him getting at least a dozen proposals from women who've fallen for him simply because he's the real deal."

Destiny had only been able to read the first three emails from women who claimed they were perfect bride material for Troy. She couldn't stomach any more. And each time, she visualized blue eyes amid black lashes, that amazing dimple, jet-black waves of hair and a smile that made her pulse skitter. "And they've only read about him. Wait until they see him."

Rita laughed. "I'm still waiting for you to send a picture. Try to take one today while you're at the fishing hole. I've searched the web, but the guy hasn't got a single photo online. No Facebook page either. I did run across some articles in the *Claremont News* from ten years ago. He was a star running back at his high school. Did you know that? The paper said a few colleges were looking at him, but then I didn't see information saying he took a football scholarship or anything like that."

Destiny thought about telling her friend she shouldn't stalk him online, but then she remembered… she'd done the same thing. And every other woman in the country probably would, too, when she revealed the name behind the guy who had been diligently looking for his wife for fifteen years.

"I think the readers would love it if you'd give them another teaser. Oh, and the one you did this morning has been a hit, too. Lots of folks commenting on how they enjoyed reading about the couple that own the five-and-dime, how they met and are still together. We even got a comment from Lamont Sharp."

Now that got Destiny's attention. "Lamont Sharp? The editor?" She remembered the influential guy speaking at her graduation from the University of Georgia. He was so impressive, so successful, so... intimidating. She'd stammered over introducing herself and then given him one of her new business cards for her online magazine. He'd actually kept the card. Not only that, but he'd commented, too? "What did he say?"

"He said the article about the couple was impressive and that it was nice to hear about a love that lasts." She paused. "It's rare nowadays, isn't it, for a couple to pull it off?"

"Pull what off?" Destiny was still thrown by the fact that Lamont Sharp—*the* Lamont Sharp—read her article and liked it.

"Marriage, the whole 'till death do us part' thing. My mom said when she was little, they were always going to anniversary parties, a twenty-fifth or a fiftieth, but I've never even heard of one happening for anyone we know. My grandparents are divorced, my parents, too. I've only got one aunt and uncle who are still married, and this is a second marriage for both of them. Kind of sad that hardly anyone gets it right the first time, huh? Pretty cool that your folks did."

Destiny slowed the car. Her parents *were* still together. Granted, it was a strained relationship, since her father always worked and her mother always seemed miserable. But they were sticking it out, and every now and then, when they did spend a decent amount of time together—like for vacations and holidays—they still seemed very much in love. And those times, Geneva Porter actually looked happy. "Yeah, pretty cool."

"Do you think it's the whole God thing that makes a difference?" Rita asked. "I mean, Troy talks about it in all of his letters, how important his faith is. Maybe the marriages that make it are because they've got that. They want to do it the right way, so they work things out instead of throwing in the towel. I know my parents never went to church. Your parents did though, right?"

"Mom dragged us to church every Sunday, if you can count that. Daddy usually had to work, but he'd make an effort to go with us on Christmas and Easter."

"Well, I may try church again. Who knows? Maybe I'd meet someone like Troy Lee."

"Maybe so." Destiny knew every girl wanted to meet someone "like Troy Lee." So did she. But unfortunately, now that she'd met him, she suspected that no other guy would ever compare to the real deal. She drove past another vast cotton field as she looked for the next dirt road, hopefully the one that led to the fishing hole.

When she called the sporting goods store this morning for directions to the place, Troy's grandfather had said she wouldn't be able to miss it. Had she missed it? She hoped not, because she was eager and ready to spend a little time with the real deal. No, she wasn't what he was looking for in a wife; she knew that. But maybe she could pretend she was for a little while…and in the process, get the rights to publish those letters.

Throughout his work routine at the fishing hole, Troy's mind hovered between how to get to know

Destiny better and how to back off from Haley. Performing his Saturday morning ritual, he'd already distributed fishing gear to several guests and cut the grassy bank on the far side of the pond, and was now running the Weed Eater around their tiny store. But every activity had been performed on autopilot, with Troy merely going through the motions while he concentrated on both girls. And his uncanny attraction to Destiny Porter.

He'd always assumed he would know when he met the right one because she would emanate every quality he'd described throughout years of writing. But he didn't know enough about the Atlanta lady to say whether she had all of the qualities he wanted in a wife. He simply knew that he couldn't stop thinking about her.

Absorbed in his thoughts, he nearly didn't hear his grandmother's yell from the store's porch. However, her wild arm wave caught his attention and had him shutting off the Weed Eater. "You need me?"

Typically she stayed busy inside the store cooking chicken fingers and her delicious pies for the guests to purchase throughout the day. Rarely did she come out to find Troy…unless she needed help. But he couldn't imagine that she'd need any help with the cooking.

"I wanted to know if you invited that sweet Haley to come out here today." She held a hand to her chest and gasped between words, and Troy felt a little guilty; how long had she been screaming at him before he'd noticed?

"I thought about inviting her, but she said she had to work. She's answering the house calls for Dr. Sheridan today." That was the truth; he'd thought about inviting Haley out to the fishing hole, right up until the moment that he realized he couldn't get his mind off Destiny. But he wouldn't tell his grandma that.

"Oh." Her disappointment filled the word, then her brows lifted and she asked, "What do you mean, answering house calls? Like if someone has a sick cat or dog at their house, she goes to check on them?"

"Or a horse or cow," he said with a grin.

Still frowning, she turned when a puff of smoke in the distance signaled that a car had started up the dirt road leading to the fishing hole. "Looks like we've got another customer." She shielded her eyes with her hand and squinted to see their new arrival, then her frown quickly converted to an all-out smile. "Well, lookie there, it's the writer! Troy, put that Weed Eater back in the shed and dust yourself off a little. Go on, I'll keep her occupied until you're more presentable."

Troy was baffled. Had she already suspected he wanted to make a good impression? "More presentable?"

"We want her to put our place in one of her books, remember? Now you'll need to show her around and make sure that she catches plenty of fish. And point out all of the flowers we've got blooming. I've planted a bazillion bulbs. Boy, I wish she'd have come in the spring when the tulips were going full blast. That would have been a real sight for her to see, but we'll do what we can, now, won't we? We've still got the daylilies going strong. Point those out to her, okay?"

Troy grinned. Leave it to his grandmother to ask him to make a good impression on the girl he was

OFFICIAL OPINION POLL

Dear Reader,

Since you are a book enthusiast, we would like to know what you think.

Inside you will find a short Opinion Poll. Please participate in our Poll by sharing your opinion on 3 subjects that are very important to all of us.

To thank you for your participation, we would like to send you **2 FREE BOOKS** and **2 FREE GIFTS!**

Please enjoy them with our compliments.

Sincerely,

Pam Powers

For Your Reading Pleasure...

Get 2 FREE BOOKS that will lift your spirits and reinforce important lessons about life, faith and love!

Free

Your 2 FREE BOOKS have a combined cover price of $11.98 or more in the U.S. and $13.50 or more in Canada.

Peel off sticker and place by your completed Poll on the right page and you'll automatically receive 2 FREE BOOKS and 2 FREE GIFTS with no obligation to purchase anything!

We'll send you two wonderful surprise gifts, (worth about $10), absolutely FREE, just for trying our Love Inspired® books! Don't miss out — MAIL THE REPLY CARD TODAY!

Visit us at:
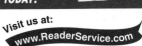
www.ReaderService.com

YOUR OPINION POLL
THANK-YOU FREE GIFTS INCLUDE:

▶ **2 LOVE INSPIRED® BOOKS**

▶ **2 LOVELY SURPRISE GIFTS**

▶ **DETACH AND MAIL CARD TODAY!** ▶

OFFICIAL OPINION POLL

YOUR OPINION COUNTS!
Please check TRUE or FALSE below to express your opinion about the following statements:

Q1 Do you believe in "true love"?

"TRUE LOVE HAPPENS ONLY ONCE IN A LIFETIME."
○ TRUE
○ FALSE

Q2 Do you think marriage has any value in today's world?

"YOU CAN BE TOTALLY COMMITTED TO SOMEONE WITHOUT BEING MARRIED."
○ TRUE
○ FALSE

Q3 What kind of books do you enjoy?

"A GREAT NOVEL MUST HAVE A HAPPY ENDING."
○ TRUE
○ FALSE

YES! I have placed my sticker in the space provided below. Please send me the **2 FREE** books and **2 FREE** gifts for which I qualify. I understand that I am under no obligation to purchase anything further, as explained on the back of this card.

❏ I prefer the regular-print edition
105/305 IDL F5HY

❏ I prefer the larger-print edition
122/322 IDL F5HY

FIRST NAME

LAST NAME

ADDRESS

APT.#

CITY

STATE/PROV.

ZIP/POSTAL CODE

Offer limited to one per household and not applicable to series that subscriber is currently receiving.

LI-TF-13

Printed in the U.S.A. © 2013 HARLEQUIN ENTERPRISES LIMITED.
® and ™ are trademarks owned and used by the trademark owner and/or its licensee.

crushing on. "I'll do my best." And he would, not only for the sake of the fishing hole, but for himself, too.

"That's real good. Oh, I'm going to take those pies out of the oven. And then I've got a little errand to run, but I won't be gone long. Everything in here will be fine. Nothing in the oven but those pies. You just spend some time with Miss Porter and show her how good the fishing is."

"I'll do that." He placed the Weed Eater in the shed beside the store and then turned to see Destiny pull her car into a parking space. She had the top down on the convertible and her dark hair pulled back in a ponytail. Small pearl earrings dotted each ear. She got out of the car and Troy noticed her outfit, a white short-sleeved button-up blouse and cuffed jean capris. Like the other night, she wasn't overdressed but still looked classy, portraying a girl from the nicer side of the tracks. Big city.

He glanced down at his dusty jeans and faded black T-shirt. What would a girl like that ever see in a country guy from the sticks?

"Hey." Destiny's bright smile seemed to shoot straight to his heart, and he felt as though he was smiling right back…from the inside. Problem was, the outside forgot to catch up because she looked confused. "It is still okay for me to visit today, right? I really would like to learn to fish."

He shook off his apprehension and answered, "Of course." Troy couldn't remember ever being nervous around a girl, but he was now. What if he got to know her, realized that she was indeed the person he'd been writing to all this time, and then learned she wasn't interested in a small-town guy without a fancy car, snazzy clothes or a four-year degree?

"Was that your grandmother I saw as I drove up?" She stepped onto the porch and peeked in through the side window. "I want to say hello."

"Yes, that's her, and I'm sure she'd like that. She got all excited when she saw your car. She's still convinced you need to put the fishing hole—and everything else about Claremont—in a book."

She laughed, knocked on the door, then peeked inside. "Hey, Mrs. Bowers."

Troy listened to them exchange small talk, his grandmother chattering nonstop in her excitement at having Destiny here. While they visited, Troy selected a couple of bamboo poles from the rack on the porch and prepared to take the lady fishing. He found himself relaxing a little with her friendly tone and with the way she seemed to fit right in to her surroundings, talking to his grandmother about her favorite kinds of pies and about how she believed that Southern cooking simply tasted better than anywhere else she'd visited.

He wondered where all Destiny had visited and assumed she'd probably seen a good portion of the States, if not the world. Troy had never been farther north than Gatlinburg or farther south than Destin. And truth be told, he didn't have to travel to find contentment. Everything he wanted or needed was right here in Claremont.

Everything, that is, except for the woman he'd been writing to for the past fifteen years. Then again, maybe she was here now. And—he smiled as Destiny laughed at something his grandmother said—maybe she'd decide she liked it here.

Still grinning, Destiny backed out of the doorway. "I'll definitely try all of it for lunch. I never turn down food."

He noted her athletic build, not too thin but definitely not heavy. "Well, you don't eat a whole lot, I'm sure," he said as she shut the door and turned to face him.

"I bet I'd surprise you. My father always said that while he may not have had a son, at least he had a daughter who ate like one."

He laughed. "I'll believe that when I see it."

"Don't worry, after smelling everything your grandmother has got cooking in there, come lunchtime, I'll show you exactly how well I put food away."

"All right. You do that." Troy liked it when a girl was comfortable enough to eat around him. The majority of them picked at their food on dates or said they weren't hungry at all. Haley hadn't eaten much last night at dinner, but that seemed more to do with the fact that her mind stayed on her work. She'd talked so much about the animals she'd tended that she barely made a dent in her lasagna. It was refreshing to hear about a woman who enjoyed a good meal, and he suddenly wanted another dinner date…but with Destiny. Today, however, until he figured out how to get this relationship going, a picnic lunch of his grandmother's cooking would have to do.

The front door opened and his grandmother bounded onto the porch, her purse draped over her shoulder, car keys in one hand and a water bottle in the other. "The pies are cooling." She looked at Destiny. "We're so glad you got to come out today. Troy's going to make sure you catch some fish. And there are a couple of other families already fishing on the other side of the pond if you want to talk to them and see how they like the experience and everything, in case you want to write about it sometime."

"That sounds great."

"Good deal. I've got a little errand to run, but I'll be back soon. Troy, don't worry about the store. Just head on out to fish with Destiny. If you see someone drive up, you can get them their gear, but I really want Destiny to get a feel for the fishing hole for her books." She'd started a tiny sprint to her car as she spoke, and she punched the key fob and then jumped in. "Y'all have fun!"

"We will," Troy promised.

Destiny watched as his grandmother stomped the gas and left a cloud of dust in her wake. "Wow, she has so much energy."

"Yes, she does. And did you notice she now has you writing *books?* Plural. Before you leave town, she'll have you penning an entire series about Claremont."

She laughed again, and Troy enjoyed the sound. "Maybe my series on Claremont will be a bestseller. I guess I should get started writing it, shouldn't I?"

"Maybe you should." He nodded toward the back. "Come on, I've got our fishing poles, but we'll need to grab some bait."

Her smile dipped a little. "Just what kind of bait? Not that I care, but I'm curious."

Oh, she was cute. "Crickets work best for bream fishing."

"And that's what we're fishing for? Bream?"

"That's what we're fishing for." They stepped around the back of the store, which had been fairly quiet until they made an appearance. Now all of the crickets went berserk, each one trying to out chirp the next guy. "They get excited when they have visitors."

She stayed a couple of steps behind Troy but peered past him toward the container he lifted, already filled with crickets and ready to go. "Because they know visitors mean they're about to become a fish's lunch?" she asked.

"Naw, I think they're just like everyone else around here and like company. Southern hospitality and all. They don't have any idea about their future on a bream's menu."

"I'll be sure not to tell them." She pointed to a stack of patchwork quilts on the porch. "Are those for picnics?"

"Picnics and fishing. The bank is grassy, but the quilt provides a little more padding against the ground. You want to pick one out for us?"

"Sure." She thumbed through the stack. "They're all so gorgeous. I wouldn't think your grandmother would want them on the ground."

"She's in a quilting group that meets at the church each week. They make more quilts than they know what to do with. Even giving them to folks for every wedding, baby and any other occasion they can think of, they still have plenty left. If you ask me, they get together for the socializing, and the quilts are merely a bonus."

Destiny withdrew a cream-colored quilt with a pale blue-and-yellow design and draped it over her arm. "The patterns are so elaborate."

"Each pattern symbolizes something, and she'll be happy to tell you what, but I have no clue what most of them mean."

"So I'm guessing she's made one or two for you?" she asked, as they walked away from the store and toward the pond.

"My hall closet is filled with quilts she made, and a few that were made by my great-grandmother. She quilted, too. My mom knows how, but she doesn't get into it nearly as much as my grandmother."

"That's amazing. So if the patterns mean something, do the quilts that she gave you have some kind of meaning for you?"

Troy had never really thought about it. He guessed the patterns symbolized something, but he'd never asked why she'd given him certain ones. "I suppose all of them do, but the one that stands out the most is the one she gave me for my high school graduation. She made it with fabric from the jerseys of every sport I'd played, from T-ball all the way up to high school football." He grinned. "That one definitely means something to me. Best gift I got." He continued walking, taking a few steps down the hill toward the pond, but then noticed she'd stopped. When he turned, he found her rubbing her hand across the bumpy fabric of the quilt, her upper teeth grazing her lower lip and her eyes apparently blinking back tears. "Destiny?"

"A quilt made by your grandmother was your best graduation gift." She visibly swallowed and looked at him with such tenderness that Troy was afraid she'd misunderstood.

"Hey, I got a lot of things that cost more, some pretty expensive gifts, I'd say. So don't feel like I didn't get all that much because I said the quilt was the best one. It's just that—" he shrugged "—because of the time she put into it and because of each fabric having meaning to me from different stages of life, it became my best gift."

She smiled, and the action caused a tear to crest over the lower edge of her eye and trickle down her cheek. Brushing it away with her hand, she explained, "I wasn't feeling sorry for you. I'm just touched that as a high school senior you realized how special the quilt was. Most people wouldn't get it, especially not that young. I think at this stage of my life, I'd appreciate the sentiment behind the present, but back then I wouldn't have." She tilted her head and studied him for a moment. "You've always been like that, haven't you? Putting a lot of thought into things and understanding what's really valuable in life."

He grinned. "Not sure how you got all of that from me saying the quilt was my best gift, but hey, I'll take it."

She chewed that lower lip again, looking as though she'd said something wrong. "It just seems like that's the way you'd be, if you liked that gift the best."

Troy nodded and wasn't bothered by her assumption. "I guess you've pegged me, though it usually takes people some time to get to know me before they figure out that I'm one of those big sappy guys who tears up when I watch a chick flick."

She grinned. "*Steel Magnolias* do you in?"

"We're not even gonna talk about it. I was pathetic."

Her laugh warmed his soul. She'd really figured out quite a lot about him already, even though they hadn't spent much time together. He longed to find out as much about her, and he hoped to do it today. Starting right now. "So what was your best gift?"

"I'm almost embarrassed to say, but since you're sharing, I will, too." She inhaled deeply, let it out. "Okay, for high school graduation, my parents gave me exactly what I asked for, a trip to Hawaii with my friend Rita."

He whistled. "That sounds pretty special to me."

"I thought it was at the time. But now, all we have are the pictures from the trip, and that's it. Then for college graduation, they gave me what I asked for again, which was money to start my own business. Mom wasn't happy about it, and she keeps reminding me that I wasted it—" she paused "—that I'm wasting my life, in her opinion."

They'd reached the large willow tree that provided the best shade on the bank and, consequently, the best fishing. Troy needed a little time to make sure he spoke wisely. Her comment about her mother had opened a small door, and he planned to step through it with caution, so he nodded toward the moss-covered ground. "Why don't you spread the blanket out there?"

Still looking disheartened, she unfolded the quilt and waved it to catch a little breeze before guiding it to the ground. Then she sat down and looked out across the pond. "It's so peaceful here, isn't it?"

Troy placed the noisy crickets by the tree trunk, then put the fishing poles beside the quilt before sitting near her. He didn't rush into getting ready to fish but instead joined her in taking in the serenity of the place.

God, give me the right words here, please. I can feel my heart pulling toward her, and I want to help her now. She may have been given a lot of things in her life, but I can sense she's missed out on even more.

He could tell there was friction with her mother, and he hated that. Family squabbles could weigh you down, especially if you feel you've disappointed your family. He knew what that was like, but he also knew how great it felt once you worked things out. Maybe his experience could help Destiny. "Your business that you started, was that with your writing?"

She nodded. "I'm writing on my own now. It isn't the fact that I've chosen writing as a profession that bothers her, but that I haven't submitted anything to a publisher and tried to get my work in front of more people." She sighed. "Or I assume that's what bothers her. We don't talk a lot." She shook her head. "Or rather we talk a good bit, but we don't say all that much."

Troy understood. "Back when I graduated from high school, my family wanted me to go to college. I'd gotten a few scholarship offers to play ball, and they wanted me to take one."

Her eyes were still moist, making the bright blue glisten in the morning sun. She focused on his words and seemed to realize that he'd been in a situation not all that different from hers. "But you didn't?"

He shook his head. "We've got a big family, and because of that, we always had a lot of vehicles around. Cars, trucks, tractors, hay balers, you name it. I started tinkering around with them when I was barely big enough to hold a wrench, and I knew in my heart that that's what I wanted to do, work on engines, make things run. What I really love is to bring an old one back to life again, give something that's past its prime a new reason to shine."

She ran her hand along the length of her ponytail, curling the tip around her fingers, and Troy found himself wondering whether that chocolate lock was as silky as it looked. "So you turned down the scholarship and started working at the filling station?"

Troy took his attention away from her ponytail. "Not to start with. I wanted to make sure that when I started working, I knew what I was doing, so I got a two-year degree from the trade school in Stockville and fine-tuned my skills, made sure I knew what was what about all types of vehicles. And then I talked to Bo and Maura about the potential of buying the business."

Her eyes widened. "*Buying* the business? You own the mechanic shop by their station?"

Troy had always felt good about his investment, but never as much as right now, hearing more than a hint of admiration in Destiny's question. But he didn't want her to overestimate his achievement. "Well, I don't own it yet, but I'm working on it." He'd been making extra payments, in fact, and should own it outright by this time next year.

"Troy, that's wonderful. And I'm guessing that when your family saw how well you were doing at the station, then they were okay about you turning down those scholarships?"

"I think they were okay once they saw that I was happy without going off to college. For some reason they all assumed that in order to feel successful, I'd need to move away from Claremont." He grinned. "Not sure where they got that, since they're all still here."

"The thing is," she whispered, then cleared her throat and continued, "my mom's right, at least partially. My big, pie-in-the-sky dream is to have a book published by a big publisher, to see something I've written in a brick-and-mortar store, instead of only online." She looked at Troy and one corner of her mouth lifted. "But if I admitted that to her, then she'd have that much more ammunition against my current online venture."

"Your writing is online?"

She nodded. "It's a digital magazine, and it's doing okay. And I'm the owner, my own boss, which is nice. Rita, my friend I mentioned, works with me and does an amazing job."

"I'll be honest. I don't think I've ever viewed an online magazine. I'm sure that's the way things are going, everything digital and all, but I really don't spend a whole lot of time on the internet. I usually get on long enough to order whatever I need for the shop, maybe pull up information on how to service a vehicle I haven't worked on before, but that's pretty much it. I don't suppose your magazine would have any of that type of information, huh?"

"No, we publish stories about—" she paused "—relationships."

"That's why you wanted to write about Marvin and Mae," Troy reasoned.

"Yes. Our subscribers enjoy hearing love stories." She reached toward a long sliver of grass, snapped it from the ground and then ran it between her fingers. "Marvin and Mae's story was popular with our readers, and I enjoy sharing stories like that…." Her voice drifted off.

"But you'd like to have a real book of yours to hold."

She nodded, then grinned. "However, should you ever meet my mother, you probably shouldn't mention that."

"Noted." He watched the sliver of grass move as she rolled it between her fingers and knew her mind was somewhere else, probably on her family. Troy didn't know enough about that situation to ask, but he'd never known of time spent fishing that didn't coincide with time spent confiding. And he wanted Destiny to confide in him, wanted to know as much as he could about the lady. "You ready to fish?" he asked.

She peered out over the pond at the families on the other side. "Yes," she said with a smile. "I bet they're all wondering why we're taking so long getting started, huh?"

"Nah, lots of folks come out here to enjoy the scenery. But I promised to teach you how to fish, and I'm not into breaking promises."

A look passed over her face that Troy couldn't make out, but she quickly converted it to a smile and said, "Then teach me how to fish."

Destiny watched as he reached for one of the bamboo poles. He was so comfortable here, sitting on a blanket beside the pond and telling her about his family, his job, his dreams. He was beautiful, inside and out. And the fact that she knew so much about him from his letters only drew her to him more. She'd almost let it slip, mentioning his sensitivity like someone who knew him well. But she did know him well, very well, from reading those letters. When she told him about her magazine, she'd feared he would ask her the name of her website or ask to read some of the things she'd written. But he hadn't. Probably because he'd read—and written—plenty of relationship stories of his own over the past fifteen years.

If he had, she could have mentioned that she wanted to publish love letters. But in any case, it hadn't seemed the right time. Or maybe she was too scared that he might see right through her and then this—whatever it was between them—would end.

Destiny did not want it to end.

He handed her the fishing pole and she found that her hands lingered a little longer than they should, touching his in the exchange. She realized that her heart tripped at the briefest contact with this man. Glancing up, she found that his eyes were also focused on their hands.

He exhaled thickly and smiled. "That feel okay for you?"

She assumed all bamboo poles felt the same, but she nodded. "Feels fine." More than fine, really, while he still held on.

Then he slid his hands away and withdrew a red-and-white cork from his pocket. "This will float on top of the water. When it goes under, you'll know you've got something."

"A fish, you mean." She watched his capable hands knot the cork in place.

He smiled. "Well, that's what we're hoping takes your bait."

"What else might take my bait?"

"Turtles or—" He stopped, his mouth open, then snapped it closed. "Just turtles."

"No, you were going to say something else." She scanned the water and thought about other things that might take bait. "Tell me there aren't any snakes out here."

"Haven't seen any in a while, and even if there were, I'm sure they wouldn't be interested in our crickets." He gave her what he probably assumed was a reassuring smile.

Destiny wasn't reassured. "How long is 'a while,' exactly?"

His eyes focused on hers, and for a slight moment, she was certain they lowered to her mouth. Suddenly she forgot all about snakes, and anything else, and wondered if he were going to act on his current thought. *Please.*

His eyes slowly moved back to hers, and finally he said, "I promise, I'll take care of you."

Destiny nodded, believing every word. He would take care of her, because Troy was the kind of guy who made a promise and followed through with it. Even if she didn't get a kiss, whatever had happened just now between them was pretty awesome.

Clearing his throat, he broke the intimate tension of the moment and turned to get the container of crickets. As before, as soon as the things got some attention, they got noisy.

"They're really loud, aren't they?" she asked, as he brought the mesh-covered jug nearer.

He smiled. "Don't worry. They'll hush up again after we get the ones we need." Cupping his hand over the end, he slid the cap to the side and then let one of the crawling bugs enter his waiting palm.

Destiny tried not to cringe, but she couldn't help it.

He winked at her. "You might want to turn your head while I put him on the hook."

She whipped her head to the side so quickly her ponytail smacked her opposite cheek. "Okay, tell me when you're done." He didn't do a very good job at muffling his laughter, so she said, "You're the one who told me not to look."

"I know, but I thought for a minute there you were going to sling your head right off."

"Very funny. Are you done?"

"All done," he said, and she turned to see him releasing a bug-covered hook toward the water. "You can drop it in now so you don't have to see the bait."

She plunked it in the water until the red of the cork balanced on top. "Now what?"

"Now I'll bait mine while you watch yours."

"I just watch it? I don't need to move it or anything like that? When I've seen fishing on TV, they're pretty active."

He baited his hook so quickly Destiny didn't have time to get grossed out by the cricket, and then he dropped his in a little ways from hers. "On TV, they're probably using a rod and reel and fishing for bass, or maybe even something bigger. For what we're doing, we sit and watch."

She looked at the two corks, floating peacefully on top of the water, barely moving at all. "How long does it take?"

He propped his pole on his knee and shifted his eyes from the cork to Destiny. "Just depends."

"On what?"

"On when the fish get hungry."

She still grasped her pole in both hands, figuring if a fish grabbed the bait it might give her a good run for her money, if this was anything like the fishing she saw on television. She was surprised he sounded so relaxed. Fishing was a sport, after all, which meant it took concentration. She was concentrating. Troy, however, didn't seem to be. She took a quick glance at him to verify that, as she suspected, he was totally looking at her and not even watching his cork. "Don't you need to pay attention?"

He grinned. "I am."

She felt her cheeks flush and found herself once again falling into a deep pit of longing for this guy. He was so perfect. Why did he have to have the woman he described in those letters? Because that was *so* not Destiny. She didn't have his faith. She didn't have the honesty he wanted in a woman, or she wouldn't be trying to get close enough to him to ask him to publish those letters.

"Hey," he said, and she realized she was staring.

She blinked, cleared her throat. "Yeah?"

"I think you've got one."

Destiny turned her attention from the good-looking guy beside her to her cork, which had—to her amazement—plunged beneath the water. "What do I do now?"

He laughed. "Pull it up."

She yanked the pole upward. "That's it?" she asked, as a small but fat fish hurled out of the water on the end of her line and made a beeline for Troy's face. He reached out and grabbed the thing before it smacked him.

Propping his own pole beneath his leg, he removed her fish from her line. "Nice catch, Destiny."

"Wow, that's pretty cool." She examined the silver scales with hints of yellow and green near the gills. The fish's eyes bulged prominently, as if it'd seen a ghost or something, and its gills flexed in and out like an asthmatic. "Oh, he's pretty, but he doesn't look so good. Is it going to kill him because I caught him?"

Troy smiled. "No, hold this while I show you what he can still do." He handed her his fishing pole and then kneeled forward to lower the fish to the water. Then he released it, and Destiny watched the silver scales until they disappeared. "He just needed to be back where he belonged. Good as new now."

Back where he belonged. Destiny thought about how well Troy belonged here, in the country, amid the fishing and his family and his friends. She didn't belong here, yet he was helping her to blend.

"Okay," he said, baiting her hook again while Destiny tried not to watch.

"Okay, what?" She handed him his fishing pole and then kept her eyes on her cork as it hit the water.

"Okay, what did you just think about that took all of the happiness off your face? The fish will be fine, you know. I wouldn't lie to you."

She nodded and, unable to look at him for fear he'd see through her turmoil, kept her eyes on the cork. He *wouldn't* lie to her, and that was part of the problem. The entire time she'd been in town, she'd been lying to him. "I know the fish will be fine. I guess my mind went somewhere else for a moment." A pitiful explanation, but she hoped it'd do.

"You want to talk about it? Does it have something to do with what you said earlier, about your mother thinking you're wasting your life?"

Nope, that wasn't what she'd been thinking about, but oddly enough, that was a safer subject, and Destiny decided to run with it. "It's crazy, isn't it? Twenty-six years old and still wanting my mother's approval?"

"I don't think there's any time in life when you don't want approval from your parents. I've always related it to our spiritual life. I mean, we all want approval from our Heavenly Father, too, right? Only makes sense we'd want approval from our earthly folks, as well."

And there it was, the faith he always mentioned in his letters. "Yeah, I guess it does."

"So your mother wants you to get your work in front of publishers? And you said that, even though you won't admit it to her, that's what you want, too, right?"

Destiny thought about how excited she was earlier when Rita mentioned that Lamont Sharp had read her blog. "Can I be honest with you?"

"I'd hope that you would."

She'd never confided this to anyone, not her parents, not even Rita, but she knew she could trust Troy. And she wanted him to understand her, the way she understood him. "The truth is, I'm afraid."

"Afraid to submit it?" he asked, securing his pole beneath his leg and then turning so he could focus on Destiny.

Destiny wasn't even looking at her cork anymore. She was lost in the blue depths of Troy's eyes and in the tender way he looked at her, as though nothing she could say would disappoint him. "Afraid that they would say no."

"Remember Wednesday night's lesson about Philippians?" he asked.

Destiny nodded but wasn't sure what the lesson had to do with her fear.

"Remember how Brother Henry was talking about rejoicing? Right after that verse, he brought up another that's one of my favorites." Troy paused, then said, "'Do not be anxious about anything, but in every situation, by prayer and petition, with thanksgiving, present your requests to God.'"

She knew what Troy referred to, but she'd never in her life presented a request to God. And she wasn't sure now was the best time to start. So she turned her focus back to the cork, floating peacefully in the water. Then she felt Troy's finger beneath her chin, and he gently turned her face toward his.

"You ask God for His help, tell Him to guide you when you submit your work, and He won't let you down."

"You really believe that, don't you?"

"I do."

"So, what if I ask God to help, submit my work, and then God's answer is no?"

"Then He has a better plan for you," Troy said, then glanced toward the water. "And right now, His plan involves you catching a fish."

Destiny's pole started to teeter from the fish's tugging, and she grabbed it before it fell into the pond. Yanking it up, she saw a huge fish on the end. "That one must be the daddy."

Troy caught the dangling fish and freed the flapping thing from the hook. "Actually, we call him Big Daddy. See that gold spot by his right gill? That's the way we identify him. He's the biggest bream we've got out here, and it's kind of rare for him to let himself get caught."

"So what do you think that means?" Destiny said as Troy lowered Big Daddy to the water and the fish splashed him before diving away.

"Maybe it means that you're meant to do things that some don't think are possible," Troy said.

"Like submit my work and get it published?"

"Maybe that, too, but I was thinking more along the lines of catching two big fish without me getting a single bite. Now, that should be impossible."

She started to laugh, but a loud growl from her stomach nearly drowned out the sound. "Oh, my, I think I'm hungry. You think your grandma meant for us to wait for her to get back before we eat lunch?"

"No, indeed. Besides, I'm ready to take a break from fishing, since you're killing me." He put the poles by the tree, stood and held out a hand to help Destiny to her feet. And once again, the contact with Troy, skin to skin, sent a shiver of awareness down her spine. She was enjoying this way too much, but she didn't want it to end. Rita had said that she needed to get his permission soon to publish those letters, but Destiny couldn't do it, not today. She'd enjoy the afternoon and maybe she'd find the courage to ask him tomorrow. She glanced at the guy now walking beside her toward the store. *Maybe.*

They washed up and then loaded a picnic basket with chicken fingers, potato salad, sweet tea and chocolate pie. Then they headed back to the quilt beneath the tree to enjoy their lunch. Destiny hummed her contentment through every mouthwatering bite, and Troy grinned at her enthusiasm.

"Told you I could eat," she said, polishing off the last smidgen of meringue from the chocolate pie.

"And you didn't lie. I'm pretty sure you ate more than me."

"I most certainly didn't." She poked him in the chest and tried to ignore the feeling she got from connecting with the hard plane.

He laughed, rolled onto his back and laced his hands behind his head. "Just messing with you, Destiny." Then he turned his head to look at her, and she felt the same sensation she'd had a moment ago, when she pressed her finger to his chest. "I'm enjoying spending time with you," he said.

"I'm enjoying it, too." And she was, way too much. Because she really needed to ask him about those letters, and once she did, she feared this connection that had started between them would be gone. She wasn't ready for that yet.

"Why don't we—" His words were cut short by a yodel from the store.

"Troy!" His grandmother stood on the front porch with her arms cradled around something small and black. "Can you come here? I need to tell you something!"

"I didn't hear her drive up." He stood from the quilt and reached out to help Destiny to her feet. "Guess we should go see what she needs."

Destiny followed along as he walked toward the store, where Mrs. Bowers fidgeted from one foot to the other.

"What have you got?" Troy asked. "Is that Lily's cat?"

"Well, after what you told me earlier, I decided to help you out today and I borrowed it." She turned her head as a vehicle started up the dirt road leading to the fishing hole. "Oh, my, I thought it would take her longer."

"Take who longer?" Troy asked while Destiny focused on the driver of the blue truck and knew that her one-on-one time with Troy had just ended. Haley Calhoun waved as she parked the pickup next to Destiny's Beemer.

"I was about to close the clinic when I got your call," she said to Mrs. Bowers. "We're only open until noon on Saturdays, so I'm glad you phoned when you did."

"Me, too," Troy's grandmother said. Her face had turned beet red, and she shrugged guiltily at Troy while Haley reached for the kitten in her arms.

"Is this the sick cat?" Haley asked.

"Well, now, you see, she was acting like she might be sick, poor dear. But now she seems like she's doing much better, don't you think?"

"How was she acting sick?" Haley continued, looking into the tiny cat's eyes and then gently pressing her fingers against its side. The cat purred contentedly and rubbed affectionately against her new friend.

"Well, I don't really know. Just seemed a little peaked, I guess. Maybe she needs a little rest. I can put her in the store and see if she feels better after a good nap. And since your clinic is closed for the day, maybe you could stay and relax a little while, too. Troy and Destiny have already set up a place for fishing. Would you like to fish with them? Destiny's gathering information for her books, and Troy's a fine teacher for fishing."

"I hadn't planned to go fishing, but it does sound like fun." Haley glanced from Mrs. Bowers to Troy.

"Actually, I've got all the information I needed about the fishing hole," Destiny said. "I should probably get on back to the bed-and-breakfast so I can write everything up while it's fresh." She hurriedly said her goodbyes and tried not to analyze Troy's expression too much. Did he look like he wanted her to stay, or was he ready for her to go so he could start fishing with the vet?

Destiny got into her car and attempted not to answer that question, but her phone rang, and Rita told her exactly...what she didn't want to hear.

"Hey, how'd it go at the fishing hole? Did you get the rights to print the letters?"

"Not yet." She glanced in the rearview mirror but couldn't see anything other than the dust in her wake. She'd wanted one more look at Troy, even if he was walking back to their quilt with Haley.

"Well, I need you to mail those letters back to me as soon as possible if you haven't already."

Destiny frowned. "What? Why?" She was hoping to stall another day or two. Somehow, she felt as though they were hers. She knew they weren't, and she knew she should send them back, but she hadn't been able to do it yet.

"His grandmother called again today. You know, we're lucky she doesn't actually subscribe to the magazine. She got the information for the contest from a bookstore that received one of our flyers. Can you imagine if she subscribed to the blog and read your post, and then put it together that it was her grandson? Anyway, she says she needs us to send them ASAP. She said it's extremely urgent now."

"Rita," Destiny whispered, "did she say why it was so urgent now?"

"She said that she needed to put them back where

she found them before he realizes that some are missing. She said he's going to need them soon, and she wants to make sure they're there."

"He's going to need them soon?" Destiny's mind raced. "She said that?"

"Yes, she said Troy told her he'd found the one, the woman he's been writing to, and he'll be giving her those letters soon."

"Troy told her that?" Her pulse throbbed so hard she felt it in her ears. "Did she say when?"

"Yeah, she said he told her last night."

Last night. When he went out with Haley. Destiny's throat clenched, her chest tightened and she pulled the car over. She'd never been able to drive when she cried.

Chapter Seven

Dear Bride-to-be,

Today is my twenty-second birthday. I've been
writing to you for ten years now, a minimum of
once a week for the past decade. I'll be honest, I
hadn't planned on it taking this long to find you.
I know, nowadays people typically wait awhile
before settling down, taking advantage of time
on their own to travel or establish their careers.
But you know from my previous letters that
wasn't what I'd planned. I want to be a young
husband, the kind that's still overwhelmed with
life in general and wants to share all of the new
and exciting aspects of adulthood with his wife.
And I want to be a young dad, like my dad was.
He was only twenty when he married mom and
just twenty-two when they had me. I remember
him doing everything with me—playing outside,
teaching me how to ride a bike, how to fish, how
to play ball. He coached every team I was on and
would get just as excited as all of us when we'd
win. And after my last Little League game, the

last team that he'd be able to coach for me, I saw my father cry for the first time. It didn't matter that I had four younger brothers he'd also coach. His times like that with me were ending. And he was such a part of all of it with me, and then with all of my siblings, that it hurt him as much as it hurt us when any phase of that life ended.

I want to be like that, young enough to be a big part of their lives, to celebrate their triumphs and to cry along with them when it's time to move on. But in order to become a dad soon, I'd have needed to have met you and set those wheels in motion. Falling in love with the woman I've been writing to all this time and showing you how much I want you to be a part of my world. Sometimes I think of how it will be, early marriage. Learning all of the intimacies of life and each other together. I know it's old-fashioned and hardly heard of during this day and age, but my first time will be with you. I've put too much thought and effort into finding the woman God has planned for me, and I don't want to ruin the beauty of our love by not experiencing that aspect of it with you for the first time on our wedding night.

I'm going to be honest with you again (aren't I always?) and let you know that I'm VERY anxious for that and again, that I sure didn't think it'd take me this long to find you. But it has. And oddly enough, I don't think I've even met you yet. I know that everything happens in God's time, and I'm praying that He will put you in my

life at the precise moment you should enter, and
I also pray that He'll let me know when I find
you. I know He will. He's never let me down.
Well, okay, I guess if you consider the fact that I
really wanted to be married by twenty-two, and I
honestly don't think I've met my bride yet; well,
that's a bit of a disappointment. But then I remember Jeremiah 29:11. "For I know the plans
I have for you, declares the Lord."

He does have a plan for me, and He has one
for you. Yours will involve meeting me one day.
I'd love for that to be sooner rather than later,
but time will tell. In any case, I'm hopeful that
I will find you soon, that I will love you soon
and that we'll have an exciting beginning to our
marriage, and then—hopefully, you'll feel the
same—we'll have children soon. As for me, I
wouldn't mind a honeymoon baby, but I suppose you'll have a say in that, too, won't you?
(I'm smiling. Hope you are, too.)
Until we meet,
Troy

Destiny finished reading her favorite letter and made
a silent vow never to forget a word. It'd been less than
a week since she'd met Troy and already she found herself wanting to marry the guy and have those six kids.

"I must be losing my mind. I'm not the girl these
are written to. Haley is. He said he found the one, and
she's it." Destiny folded the letter and slipped it back
in the envelope, then added it to the mailer that she'd
already prepared to send to Rita with the other let-

ters Troy's grandmother entered in the contest. Funny that she had to mail them back to Atlanta, when she could easily hand deliver them to Jolaine Bowers. But Troy's grandma had no idea that his letters were back in Claremont, or that Destiny had read each and every word of them repeatedly over the past month, until she could almost recite them by heart.

Destiny sealed the mailer, then looked up to see Mr. and Mrs. Tingle pulling in the driveway to the B and B. They waved, and Destiny lifted her hand and forced a smile. She'd grown very fond of the sweet couple over the past few days, had grown fond of everyone she'd met in Claremont. The town was like something out of an old movie, so appealing and filled with happy, friendly people.

"Did you find the breakfast casserole in the kitchen?" Annette Tingle asked as they walked toward the porch.

"Yes, I did. It was delicious, thanks."

"We were hoping you might ride to church with us this morning," Mr. Tingle said, "but when you didn't come down, we figured you either weren't feeling well or overslept."

"I overslept." Destiny would've gotten up if she had set the alarm, which she didn't. Oddly, she'd felt an urge to go to church this morning, but she didn't want to see Troy again, not yet. She needed time to process and come to grips with the fact that he'd found the girl he thought he'd marry, and time to process the aching realization that she wished it was her.

As if Mrs. Tingle knew where Destiny's thoughts had headed, she said, "Troy Lee asked about you."

"That's a nice young man, now, let me tell you." L. E. Tingle pointed a finger to emphasize the statement.

Destiny nodded. No finger point was necessary. She knew he was a nice young man. A wonderful young man. A man any girl would love to call her own, for life. And he thought Haley was the one, but still… "He asked about me?"

Mrs. Tingle gave a firm nod. "Said he had looked forward to seeing you in church this morning."

Destiny shouldn't ask the next question that popped in her head. She knew she shouldn't, but she simply couldn't help it. "Was—was Haley Calhoun, you know, the new vet, at church this morning?"

"Yes, yes, she was," Mr. Tingle said. "I actually talked to her a bit after the service to ask if she knew how we could keep the rabbits out of our garden out back, and she told me to use garlic powder."

"Garlic powder, really?" Mrs. Tingle asked, and her husband nodded.

Destiny wanted to find out if Haley had been standing next to Troy when Mr. Tingle talked to her about rabbits and garlic powder, but she didn't want to seem too interested. Instead, she glanced at the mailer in her hand. "I need to take this to the post office. Or is there a postbox nearby?"

"Would you like for us to put it with our mail going out tomorrow, dear? It wouldn't be any trouble." Mrs. Tingle offered her an easy smile.

Destiny's fingers tightened involuntarily around the mailer. She knew she could mail it from the house, but she couldn't bear handing Troy's letters over and risking someone from his town reading his innermost secrets.

She cringed. If she got his permission to run them, his innermost secrets would be on display for the entire world.

"Annette, she may want to walk to the postbox to get a little exercise since she hasn't been out yet today. There's a box outside of Nelson's Variety Store on the square."

"Yes, I would like to get out and get a little exercise," Destiny said, thankful that he gave her a way out of the uncomfortable question. She stood and started down the front porch stairs.

"Oh, that reminds me, Troy wanted me to give you a message, dear." Mrs. Tingle's words stopped Destiny in her tracks.

"A message?"

"Yes, about this afternoon. He said if you wanted to get out and do something fun today, you should go to the baseball field over at Hydrangea Park. The men's league has a game there at two and he thought you'd enjoy it. He said a few couples would be there that you might want to interview, or something like that."

"Thanks, I might." She wanted to go to the game. If there were couples there, she might score a few more stories of how they met, and after her talk with Troy yesterday she'd almost gotten the nerve to submit them for potential publication. Almost. But going to talk to the couples meant seeing Troy at the baseball field. She didn't know if she was ready to see him without letting on that her heart had fallen for the guy. And when she did see him again, she'd need to ask him for the rights to run those letters.

All in all, that didn't bode well for her taking in the baseball game.

Another wave to the Tingles and then she began the walk to the square to send away the letters that had consumed each of her days since they'd first arrived in Atlanta. Her hand gripped the mailer even tighter, already dreading the moment when she had to let them go.

The houses were still decorated for the holiday, with red, white and blue bunting draped along every porch railing and flags everywhere. Several families visited outside, the sound of children's laughter occasionally filling the air, accompanied by chirping birds. A summer breeze carried the scent of blooming flowers and fresh-cut grass. And Destiny realized that of all the places she'd ever visited, Claremont had become her favorite. She'd miss it when she had to leave, which would be later this week, she supposed. She needed to get back home to work with Rita on getting their next issue ready, the one that would include Troy's letters.

But Destiny knew she didn't have to go back so soon. That was one of the blessings of a job that was done online: she could work anywhere. However, she'd have no reason to stay once she got Troy's permission—if she got it. And she certainly didn't want to stick around to see his relationship with Haley grow.

By the time she reached the square, she'd resolved that she could do what she had to do. She'd continue to befriend Troy and then talk him into letting her run the letters, the way she'd planned when she first arrived in Claremont. Then she'd head home and maybe attempt to find a Troy Lee of her own.

As if more than one guy like him existed.

She swallowed past that bitter pill and practically stomped across the square. But when she reached the red-and-blue postbox outside of Nelson's, she hesitated. Once she put this mailer in, she wouldn't have a chance to hold the letters again, read the tender words and pretend that they were written to her and her alone. She bit her lip, opened the hinged door on the box and slowly moved the mailer to the opening.

"Hey, Destiny!"

She jumped at the sound of her name, and her hand inadvertently released the mailer into the box, the hinged door snapping shut with a loud thud and Destiny felt the loss of knowing the letters were gone.

"Oh, I'm so sorry. I didn't mean to scare you." Haley Calhoun had apparently just exited Nelson's, because she stood near the door but faced Destiny. She wore a bright pink sundress with a white cardigan, her hair pulled into a sleek ponytail and her makeup flawless.

Destiny hadn't even put on makeup yet. She hadn't thought she'd run into anyone she knew on the short walk to the square, so she still wore her tattered blue-jean shorts and navy Braves T-shirt. She never dressed this haphazardly. These were the type of clothes she wore when she knew for sure that she wouldn't be getting out of the house. Why had she put them on today?

"Hi, Haley, how are you?"

"I'm great. I came to Nelson's with some friends

from church and saw you through the window. I thought I'd see if you still wanted to talk to me about the differences between Ocala and Claremont. I've got this afternoon free, if you do." Her green eyes were bright and excited, extremely friendly, and Destiny thought about how well she'd fit into a town like Claremont, how well she'd fit into Troy's life.

Then Destiny wondered whether Troy was a part of the "friends" Haley had mentioned who were sitting on the other side of the Nelson's window. She was even more embarrassed at her outfit. "Who did you come with?"

"Mandy and Daniel Brantley, Casey Cutter, Nadia Berry and Matt and Hannah Graham. Hannah saw you, too, and was telling us that she shared the story of how she and Matt met with you. Mandy said she'd love to tell you her and Daniel's story, as well. Daniel is the youth minister at the church. I don't know how they met yet, but she said it's a good story. I'm still learning everyone around here, too, you know."

So, no Troy in the group. Destiny wondered why he hadn't come along. And then she remembered the baseball game. Maybe he had to go get ready. But in any case, she knew where he'd be at two. And she had an idea about a better way to befriend Troy and earn his trust so he'd say yes when she asked about those letters.

She'd help him get the girl he wanted.

"If you're free this afternoon, why don't we go watch the men's baseball team at two? I could talk to you about Ocala and Claremont while we watch the game, and that might give me the opportunity to interview some more couples about how they met so I can include their stories in my writing."

"That's a great idea. Mandy had asked me if I was going to the game, but I didn't know. Daniel plays on the team, too. Do you want me to meet you there, or would you like to ride together? You know where the field is?"

"It's at Hydrangea Park, not too far from the high school. I've seen the sign." Destiny had another idea to help Troy out, too, and she'd go ahead and act on it before she changed her mind. "Why don't I pick you up, and we can ride together to the game?"

Haley's smile brightened. "Sure. I only live a couple of miles down Claremont-Stockville Road, but here is the address." She withdrew a card from her purse and jotted her address on the back.

Destiny accepted the card. "I'll pick you up at one forty-five." Then she also accepted the fact that she was about to help Troy get together with his future bride.

Troy heard the crack of the bat and knew the heavy hitter from Stockville had connected well even before he saw the baseball hurtling through the air above the second baseman's head. He'd always been able to cover a lot of ground at center field, but this fly ball was headed directly between him and Daniel Brantley, playing right field.

"I got it!" Troy yelled, and then he hoped that he'd make it in time. Running with all of his might toward the fence, he kept his eye on the ball and knew he wasn't going to get there standing up…so he dived.

His body collided with the ground in a pounding thud, the skin of his forearm scraping free against the hard grass as he stretched his glove out and felt that beautiful sting of the ball colliding with his palm.

Grinning in spite of the blood seeping freely from the grazed flesh, he held up his prize and laughed at the cheers from his teammates. And then he glanced toward the stands and saw that somewhere between his last look at the bleachers and the catch of a lifetime, she had arrived. Destiny was here, and right now, she had a hand over her mouth, her eyes were wide and she'd undoubtedly witnessed the best play he'd made since high school.

Thank You, God.

"Hey, Troy, you gonna throw it back in or stand there holding it all day?" John Cutter, the pitcher, had a huge smile as he yelled. "You'd think you made a decent play or something."

Troy threw the ball in. "Same kind of play I always make, Cutter."

John's laugh filled the air, as did some teasing remarks from the rest of the players on the field. The guys had been friends and fellow athletes since they were in grade school, and their hurled insults were only a sign that they had been impressed with Troy's catch. He glanced again at the stands and hoped that Destiny was equally impressed.

And that's when he noticed Haley sitting beside Destiny. She hadn't been there before either, and the two of them were chatting as they watched the game. Troy had felt awkward after church when Haley and a few of his friends asked him to go to Nelson's for lunch. He'd hoped to see Destiny this morning and had been surprised when she hadn't shown at the service. He'd so enjoyed their time together at the fishing hole yesterday and had looked forward to sitting with her again at church this morning, had actually planned to invite her to lunch on the square after the service. He'd politely declined the invite with Haley and had hoped that he still might get a chance to spend time with Destiny today if she came to the game. Which she had done. Apparently with Haley.

Troy kept an eye on the women in the stands as best he could while also trying to show off a bit on the field. Everyone in town knew how he played in high school, but Destiny wouldn't know. He found himself working up a good sweat trying to make sure he didn't miss any fly balls headed anywhere near his vicinity in the outfield. At bat, he put so much into his swing that he hit his first home run in two years. And each time, he'd glanced toward the stands to see if she'd noticed, then he'd inwardly chastise himself for his portrayal of a male peacock displaying his feathers.

God, help me out, here. I want her to think I'm special.

By the time the game ended, Troy had caught four additional fly balls, hit a triple and then followed that with another over-the-fence homer that ended the game and sent him running the bases, all of which made him think that God was indeed helping him out. He passed third base and looked to the stands prepared to smile at the woman he believed he was falling for and saw that…she was gone.

His run slowed during the final stretch to home and

he accepted the high fives from his teammates with a smile, even though he felt the adrenaline already depleting. Destiny had left before the game ended, before he even got a chance to talk to her.

Packing up his things, he noticed Haley walking toward the dugout, her white-blond hair in a high ponytail, her green eyes sparkling, with a beaming smile. "You played a great game."

A week ago, before a little red Beemer rolled into the filling station, he'd have been thrilled to hear the compliment from Haley. Now he wished he was hearing it from someone else.

"Thanks."

"Destiny Porter came to the game, too," she said, unaware that he'd attempted to keep an eye on the lady ever since he spotted her in the stands. "I actually rode here with her, but she had to leave early to work on one of her stories."

Troy grabbed his glove. "Well, I'm glad y'all came."

"Destiny suggested that since she had to leave early, you might be willing to give me a ride home?"

He was thrown. Destiny had suggested he take Haley home? Why?

Obviously his confusion was written all over his face because Haley added, "But if you'd rather I ask someone else for a ride, I can check with Daniel and Mandy."

Troy shook his head. "No, I can take you home. No problem at all." He forced a smile and decided that, after he took Haley home, he was going to the Claremont Bed and Breakfast and getting some answers.

Chapter Eight

Destiny read through her email one more time, moved the cursor to the send button and then jerked it away. Again. She'd been battling her nerves ever since she finished writing it and still couldn't get the courage to send her work to Lamont Sharp. The attachment was there, a proposal of small-town love stories from Claremont and a pitch to write stories about additional Southern towns. The idea excited her, collecting true Southern love stories and then sharing them with the world.

But her fear was more powerful than the possibility that Lamont Sharp might actually like her proposal.

"You ask God for His help, tell Him to guide you when you submit your work, and He won't let you down."

Troy's words echoed through her thoughts, his faith in God obviously pushing away any doubt. Why couldn't Destiny find that faith?

As soon as she'd arrived home from the baseball game, she'd brought her computer and her Bible out to the front porch. She'd powered up the laptop and started composing this email, but she had yet to open the Bible that currently rested on the wicker table nearby. Reaching for it, she decided to put her priorities in the right order. She would ask God for help, and then she'd decide whether to submit her proposal to Lamont Sharp.

The Bible still felt new, the leather scent strong and the pages crisp. Since she'd rarely used it before last Wednesday night, the book opened to the exact scripture that Troy had found for her during that Bible lesson. Destiny read the verses from Philippians 4 again.

"Rejoice in the Lord always. I will say it again: Rejoice! Let your gentleness be evident to all. The Lord is near. Do not be anxious about anything, but in every situation, by prayer and petition, with thanksgiving, present your requests to God."

Troy believed those verses, and he'd told Destiny that she should, too. But could she? She put the Bible back on the table, then closed her eyes and prayed. *God, if You're listening, I'm doing what Troy said, what the Bible says, and presenting my request to You. Let me know whether I should give this a go, whether I should send this email, put my work out there and try to get it published. You know how afraid I am that it will be rejected, that essentially I will be rejected.* Destiny squeezed her eyes tighter, already feeling a little relief simply because she'd found the courage to ask God for help and believing that He listened. *If You want me to send it, then help me do it, Lord. In Jesus's name, amen.*

"Kind of an odd place to take your Sunday afternoon nap, isn't it?"

The deep baritone startled Destiny, and she jumped, her eyes popping open to see Troy, as amazingly gorgeous as ever, stepping onto the porch.

"Sorry, I didn't mean to scare you." His grin said he wasn't all that sorry, but Destiny didn't care. She really was glad he was here.

"I wasn't napping," she explained, then added quietly, "I was praying."

His look turned tender. "Another great way to spend a Sunday afternoon."

Destiny nodded, feeling pretty good about the fact that she'd found it somewhat easy to ask God about what to do, whether she should send the proposal. Glancing at her computer, she was surprised to see the email no longer displayed. "Oh, no."

"Something wrong?" He moved toward her. "Can I help?"

Destiny realized what had happened with utter clarity. When Troy startled her, she'd jumped, and apparently her hand had also moved…and inadvertently clicked the mouse over the send button. With her pulse skittering, she opened her out-box and saw that, as she feared, the proposal had now been delivered to Lamont Sharp. There was no going back.

"I asked God to help me do something," she whispered, then looked up to Troy, "and He did." Unfortunately, she wasn't sure she felt all that positive about it.

"That's usually a good thing." Troy had moved in front of her rocker and leaned confidently against the porch rail. He no longer wore his baseball uniform but had on a blue T-shirt and jeans. The blue matched his eyes, making them look almost electric, and Destiny momentarily forgot about the fact that she'd sent an unsolicited proposal to one of the biggest editors in the business.

She smiled. "Yeah, I suppose you're right." Then she remembered leaving Haley at the baseball field. "I thought you were taking Haley home."

"I did, and then I went home and got cleaned up, and then I came here." He looked at her for a moment and Destiny got the feeling he was selecting his next words carefully. She started to say something—anything—to break the awkward silence, but then he said, "Tell me something. Why did you tell Haley to ask me for a ride home? Why didn't you just take her home?"

"Because I needed to leave to work on something." She hated her defensive tone, and she also hated that she wasn't exactly telling the truth, and she was pretty sure he knew it.

"But why did you tell her to ask *me* to take her home?"

"I knew y'all went out Friday night, and then that she came to the fishing hole yesterday, so I thought you might want to spend some more time together." She made her voice sound as chipper as possible. "And that'll eliminate that player status your grandmother was worried about, you spending several days seeing the same girl. You know, maybe I could help you out with that."

He looked confused. "Maybe you could help me out with what?"

"Your player status, or I guess you'd say your relationship status, with Haley. I like her, and we got along real well today. Maybe I could spend some time with her, find out what she likes, let you know and help you develop a real relationship." Destiny couldn't believe the words coming out of her mouth.

His eyes narrowed, and he looked as though he wasn't sure what to think of Destiny's offer. She wasn't sure what to think of it either, but she'd made it, so she pushed her smile up higher. "What do you think?"

"I think I do want to build a relationship, and I definitely want to end the player reputation, even though I haven't really had a reason to earn the label."

"That's great," she said, but she couldn't manage to make her tone the least bit enthusiastic.

"But I think you're confused about what I want, and about *who* I want," he said smoothly.

She swallowed. He had something on his mind, she could see that, and she also could tell that she was a part of whatever had ticked him off. Or she guessed he was ticked off. She hadn't figured out his looks enough to tell. But he wasn't happy, for some reason. That was for sure. "I'm confused," she said.

He nodded, shifting his weight so that one shoulder rested against one of the white porch posts. "I want to ask you something, and I want you to give me an honest answer. Do you think you can do that?"

Oh, boy. Could she? Her eyes drifted to the Bible and to the memory of asking for God's help a few minutes ago. He'd want her to tell Troy the truth about whatever he was going to ask. She sure didn't want to let Him down now that she'd decided to trust Him to help. "I'll try."

"The last play of the game. Did you see it?" The corner of his mouth crooked up, and he rested a little more solidly against the porch rail as though he knew the answer but simply needed to hear it. When Destiny didn't readily answer, he repeated, "Did you, Destiny?"

She thought of that amazing home run and every other outstanding play he'd made on the field. She had attempted to chat with Haley and with all of the other people sitting around them in the stands, but it'd been hard to pay attention to the conversations because her eyes never wavered from Troy. His stance at the plate reminded her of the Braves players she watched so avidly back home. He exuded confidence in every motion, every look, and it had mesmerized her. Her desire to watch him, admire him, silently cheer him on to victory had been so unbelievably strong that she simply couldn't leave without making sure she saw every play. "I saw it."

"Where were you? Haley said you left the game right before it ended, but I didn't see you or your car anywhere. So where were you when you saw that last play?"

She looked at her computer screen, even though it merely displayed her screen saver, a photo of her and Bevvie. She couldn't look at Troy.

"Destiny?" he prodded.

She took a deep breath, knowing she had no choice but to tell the truth. "I parked at the next field for a few minutes. That was a nice home run, by the way."

"Why did you stay to see it if you had to leave and get some things done?"

Because I wanted to see you. She couldn't make her voice utter the truth, so she kept her eyes focused on the photograph and tried to remember the day it'd been taken. Last year at Thanksgiving when the family was together and everyone—even their mother—had been happy.

Troy leaned forward and eased the laptop closed so that the image disappeared. "Listen, you don't have to tell me why you stayed. I shouldn't have asked. But let me tell you what *I* was doing during the game." He waited until she had no choice but to look into those beautiful blue eyes. "I played my very best because I knew someone was in the stands that I wanted to impress."

"Haley," she whispered.

He shook his head. "No. You." The words were said with such emotion that she knew for certain he meant them.

"Me?" she whispered, and a path of goose bumps marched up her arms and legs. He'd been playing to impress *her?* "But what about Haley?"

"Haley is a nice girl, and I think we'll be good friends, which is what I told her when I took her home. I also told her that I really enjoyed my morning with you at the fishing hole yesterday and that I believed I felt a connection with you." He paused and then smiled. "That's when she told me that she believed the feeling was mutual, saying you'd barely been able to talk to her during the game because you'd been so focused on watching me."

Destiny felt her cheeks burn. "Oh, my, she must have thought I was so rude."

He laughed. "No. In fact, she said she'd already decided for herself that she was too into her job right now to be in a relationship or even to date, and she'd planned to ask me if I'd thought about asking you out." He leaned back and grinned. "I had, by the way."

"You…had." The shock of all of this truth telling was knocking her for a loop, but it was a very happy, wonderfully exciting loop.

He nodded. "Just need to find out if you'll say yes."

Every time Destiny had read Troy's love letters she'd dreamed about what it would feel like to have something so heartfelt written to her. Now, she realized, she might actually find out.

"Say yes, Destiny." His words were low and husky and sent a delightful shiver down her spine.

Troy held out his hand and held his breath as he waited for her answer. He had sensed something different about Destiny ever since that first day, with their conversation at the filling station and then their interaction that night at church. The time spent together with his family at the parade had also sparked Troy's interest. But their time together yesterday, when he got to know her more personally as they visited at the fishing hole, cemented the truth—that he felt something special toward this lady. And he suspected that God had finally answered his prayers with the woman he'd been writing to…but she still hadn't answered his question.

"Destiny? I asked you out. Are you actually going to break my heart by saying no?"

She smiled. "No."

"You're saying no?" Troy knew the answer, but he still wanted to hear it.

She ran her hand along the length of her ponytail, curling the tip around her fingers, and laughed. "No, I'm saying yes. Yes, I'll go out with you."

He loved the way she continued wrapping her hair nervously around her fingers, almost as much as he liked the way she seemed unable to control the smile that lifted her cheeks and made her eyes dance. And now, she'd said yes. Troy extended a hand. "Okay."

She slipped her hand in his and asked, "Okay, what?"

"Okay, you said I could take you out, and I figure there's no time like the present."

She glanced down at her outfit. "I'm not exactly ready for a date." She wore a pale pink T-shirt, white capris and sandals, the same outfit she'd had on at the baseball field, and she looked absolutely adorable.

"You're dressed perfectly."

She stood, then touched her face. "I'm not even wearing makeup."

"And you're beautiful," he said softly. He liked the way her cheeks flushed with the compliment. "I mean it." Troy moved closer, saw her eyelids begin to close and knew that she wanted this kiss as much as he did.

The door flew open, causing him to take a tiny step back and completely blowing the moment. Mr. Tingle carried an old-fashioned wooden ice-cream freezer while Mrs. Tingle followed close behind with two boxes of ice-cream salt nestled in one arm and a couple plastic bags of groceries hanging from the other.

"Oh, hello, Destiny," Mrs. Tingle said. "Troy, I didn't know you were here." She eyed the two of them and apparently realized, or at least suspected, what she'd interrupted. "Well, I'll be." Then she cleared her throat and attempted to hide her smile. "Oh, ah, Troy, how are you?"

"I'm fine." He smiled in spite of the fact that the sweet lady had just blown his first kiss with Destiny. "You want me to help you carry that?"

"Oh, no, dear, I've got it." She bumped the door closed with her hip. "If you take something now, you'll throw me off balance. Are you two coming to the ice-cream social? Doesn't start for another hour, but L.E. and I are going early to make sure our ice cream is ready in time."

Destiny had looked a little embarrassed when the couple first came out, but she seemed at ease now. "Ice-cream social?"

"At Hydrangea Park," Mrs. Tingle said. "One of the best events we have all year, if you ask me. The church always has an ice-cream social at the park on the Sunday closest to the Fourth of July. And that's today. We'll have a Bible study first, and then everyone eats ice cream. L.E. and I are making our Orange Crush ice cream. You really should come and try it."

Troy looked to Destiny. "Would you like to go?"

"It sounds like fun."

"We'll be there," he said.

The lady stopped walking, studied Troy and Destiny, then tilted her head and smiled. "I like the idea of you dating Destiny, Troy. She'll be good for you." Then she shifted her attention to Destiny. "He's got a reputation of being a player, or that's what the ladies at the quilting group say, just so you know. I don't believe it, mind you, but I figured I should tell you." She nodded knowingly.

Troy laughed. "Are there any secrets left in this town?"

"None that haven't made it to the quilting group, dear." And with that parting remark, she headed toward their car, where L.E. waited beside her door. She got in, and he shut the door, then looked back toward the porch.

"Can't keep much from that quilting group." He shrugged, rounded the car, climbed in and then they left.

Troy noted the shocked look on his date's face. "Might as well get used to people telling you exactly what they think. That's the way things are around here." He expected her to smile, but she instead looked troubled. "What is it?" he asked.

"It sounds like you think I'll be staying around here awhile. What happens when I need to go back home?" She visibly swallowed and worry etched her features. "I want to go out with you, but…"

He'd been thinking the same thing, ever since he realized that he had serious feelings for the writer. But he didn't want the fact that she lived two hours away to affect the possibility of him finally finding the girl he'd been writing to. And he wasn't going to let anything stop him from seeing if his suspicion was true, that Destiny was the one. "You want to go out with me, right? And see where these feelings can take us?"

"Yes, I do." She started to say more, but Troy pressed a finger to her lips to stop her progress.

"Then let's concentrate on that, going out and getting to know each other better. We'll cross any other bridges when we get to them. Right now, I want to take you on our first date, and it appears that date will end with an abundance of ice cream."

"Okay." Her smile warmed his heart. "If it ends with ice cream, how does it begin?"

"With this." He stepped closer, tenderly brushed his fingers along her jaw, then gently cupped her face. Her eyelids, as before, slid closed, and this time, no one interrupted. Troy took his time, touching his lips to hers and enjoying the soft warmth of their first kiss. He'd known he felt something special toward Destiny, but he was still overwhelmed by the emotion that accompanied the kiss, a feeling as if he never wanted this closeness, this amazing feeling, to end.

Apparently his emotion got the best of him because the kiss eventually ended with Destiny's giggle against his lips.

He grinned. "I'm guessing I crossed the typical first kiss boundary there, huh?"

She laughed. "Unless you always have people honking car horns when you kiss."

Troy vaguely remembered the sound, but it hadn't been enough to make him stop. "Nope, that's a first." Smiling, he nodded toward his truck. "We should probably leave so we can get to the social." *And so I can get away from the desire to kiss you again, right now, but longer.* He'd waited fifteen years to meet this girl. Now he'd have to keep his emotions in check, and that probably meant limiting their time alone, for the time being.

"Okay." She placed her hand in his, her smaller fingers sliding easily between his larger ones.

Troy liked the way their hands fit together, he liked the way they fit together, and he looked forward to getting to know more and more about Destiny Porter, the woman who, he believed, God had sent to Claremont...and to him. In his mind, he knew that his life was now complete, perfect.

What could possibly go wrong?

Chapter Nine

"**D**estiny, you've got to ask him about those letters. We only have four days until we're supposed to put out the next issue, and we don't have anything else to use. The advertisers are expecting it. Our subscribers are expecting it, too." Rita waited, as she had waited every other day for the past two and a half weeks, but Destiny couldn't give her the answer she wanted.

Each day Destiny promised her friend that she'd try to get Troy's permission to publish the letters, but so far, he still hadn't even told her about them. And what's more, now she firmly believed that he'd eventually give the letters to her, as his future bride. She couldn't hold back her excitement at that thought.

"Destiny, please," Rita pleaded. "You've got to help me out here. You said you would ask him last night. That's what you told me yesterday morning."

"I said I would *try* to ask him," Destiny clarified, "but I didn't. I couldn't. And," she knew she had to tell Rita the truth, "I don't think I can."

The sound Rita emitted was almost a growl. "We promised our readers. And we promised our advertisers, too!" Frustration punctuated each word. "If we don't deliver, I don't see how anyone will continue reading, and I know advertisers won't stay on board if we don't follow through with our promises. You know this, Destiny. What has gotten into you?"

Love, that's what's gotten into me. Destiny withdrew a daisy from the vase of fresh flowers Troy had brought her this morning before he went to work. He'd brought her flowers each morning since that first date to the ice-cream social, and they'd shared breakfast every morning on the B and B's porch. Then Destiny spent her day writing about love, in particular the love stories she'd learned from the couples around Claremont. Mr. and Mrs. Tingle seemed to enjoy watching the bond between Destiny and Troy growing each day and didn't mind feeding Troy as well, each morning.

His day started and ended at the bed-and-breakfast now, since he was also there every night to spend time with Destiny, take her for walks to the square or along for his baseball practices at Hydrangea Park, and then they'd return for an intimate Bible study on this porch.

Destiny had never read the Bible as much as she had in the past two weeks, but she'd grown to enjoy the daily devotions with the man she loved. And she honestly believed their relationship was stronger because of it. Last night he'd shown her a new verse in Ecclesiastes that talked about a cord of three strands that wasn't easily broken, and then he'd said their love was like a cord of three strands, composed of Troy, Destiny and God.

She simply couldn't ruin everything by asking him to publish those letters. "We just need to come up with something else to publish this time. I'll write up some text for the issue today."

Rita's exasperated breath huffed through the line. "They want the letters. You said you'd publish them, Destiny, and you need to follow through. It'd be different if we had decent backup letters to publish, but the second-place letters weren't nearly as intriguing. Plus, with the teasers we've given about Troy, no one else's letters would live up to the hype." She waited a beat then added, "As your friend and, more importantly, as your managing editor, I'm telling you that if you don't put those letters out the way you said you would, you might as well kiss the magazine goodbye. And then what will you do to make a living? You and I both know your savings are almost gone, and if our advertisers and subscribers leave, you won't have any income. I've got my other job waitressing to help me make ends meet, but what will you do?"

Destiny held the daisy to her nose, inhaled, and prayed, *God, please, help me work all of this out.*

"You can't live on love," Rita said flatly. "It sounds great in theory, and I'm thrilled that you've found someone you've fallen for, but that's not going to pay the bills."

Destiny knew her friend was right. She'd mailed the check for the August rent on her Atlanta apartment this morning, paid the Tingles for another week at the B and B, and then realized that, at the rate she was going, her bank account would hit bottom in two weeks.

"Maybe I should try to find a job in Claremont," she said aloud, which was a mistake with Rita still on the line and listening. "I saw an advertisement on the window of the *Claremont News* looking for a reporter. Maybe I could write for the paper."

"What? Destiny, you've only been dating him a few weeks. You don't know where this relationship will head. Do you really think you want to give up everything and move to the middle of nowhere?"

"What am I giving up? I can run the magazine from here."

"But this is Atlanta. You're used to the city, the fast pace. Are you really ready to settle down with, what, ten thousand people?"

"Forty-five hundred," Destiny corrected, remembering the hand-painted number displayed on the welcome-to-Claremont sign at the town's entrance.

Rita's groan was nearly inaudible but still made it through the line. "I know he's special. I get that from his letters. But what if those other people down there are right? You said they think he's a player. What if he is?"

"They thought he was—" Destiny grinned at the ridiculousness of it "—but now they've seen that he can date someone and get serious—very serious—with her. His grandmother told me that even her quilting group believes his player days are over." She laughed, thinking about the sweet lady and her adorable group of friends. They were right; Troy's "player" days were over, and Destiny thanked God every day that she was on the receiving end of his love. She couldn't wait until she could read each and every one of those letters… because they were meant for her.

"Those love letters could save us, and you know

it." Rita's words were more of a desperate plea now, and Destiny hated hearing her so upset.

"I'm sorry. I am. And I still think I can come up with something that will appease our subscribers and our advertisers for this issue. I'm going to pray about it."

"*Pray* about it?"

She wished her friend would believe in the power of prayer as much as she did now, thanks to Troy. "Yes, Rita. And I've come to believe that prayer works."

"I don't even want to get started arguing with you about that. Not sure what would happen to me if I discounted the possibility, so I'm not going there. But I do want you to think about this—if Troy Lee loves you as much as you say he does, then he should be willing to help you save your magazine by letting you publish those letters."

Destiny put the daisy back in the vase with the other flowers. She had actually considered asking Troy about the letters, but that would reveal the fact that she'd come to Claremont because of them. She knew Troy loved her, but she didn't know if their new love was strong enough to survive the fact that she'd originally lied to him about why she'd come to Claremont. Plus, there was another reason she didn't want to publish those letters.

She didn't want to share *her* letters with the world.

"I'm not going to ask him, Rita. But I'll come up with something else to publish. We're not going to stop producing the magazine. We'll give them something a little different than what they expect, that's all."

"A little different? How do you plan on finding

something a *little* different? Oh, wait. I remember. You're going to pray about it."

Destiny refused to let Rita's irritation ruin her day. She was going to pray for help, and God would grant her request, the way Troy believed He did, and the way she now believed He did, too. "Yes, I am." Her phone beeped with another call, and she glanced at the display to see her mother's name. "Hey, that's my mom. I need to let you go."

"Wow, I know you don't want to talk to me when you let me go to talk to your mom. But I can take the hint. Call me when your prayer time gives you some form of an answer. I won't hold my breath." She disconnected, and Destiny clicked over to the other line.

"Hi, Mom."

"Hi, Mom? I haven't heard from you in over two weeks, and you answer with 'Hi, Mom'?"

Destiny had expected this. No, she hadn't called her mother since the day they'd discussed her sister's engagement, but her mother hadn't attempted to call her either. However, as usual, Destiny was at fault for the lack of exchange. She thought of Troy, and of the way he got along so well with his family, and she wanted to make an effort to have that kind of relationship with her mother, too. *Help me out here, God. Let us have a conversation without fighting, please.*

Destiny took a deep breath then gave her mother the response she wanted. "I'm sorry. I should have called. It's just that I've had a lot of things going on here, and I didn't think about calling."

Her mother's gasp came through the line loud and clear, but then she cleared her throat and seemed to process the fact that, probably for the first time ever, Destiny had given her an apology. "Well, you should have called," she paused then added, "but I understand."

Surprised at the calmness of her tone, Destiny said a quick thank-you to God. This prayer thing was more powerful than she'd realized. Her mother had no lashing out, no reminders that Destiny had disappointed her parents with her career choice, no demands that she come back to Atlanta this instant. In other words, this wasn't a typical Geneva Porter phone call, and suddenly Destiny wondered if something was wrong. "Mom, is everything all right?"

Her mother's laughter filled the line. "Oh, now, isn't that terrible, that if I'm not yelling at you, you assume something is wrong?"

Destiny laughed as well, because it was true. "I'm sorry. I guess I'm not used to us talking without a fight." *Thank You again, God, for saying yes.*

Her mother paused a moment, then whispered, "Well, then, I'm the one who should be sorry."

"It's okay, Mom. Takes two to fight, you know."

"Yes, I know. But I don't like fighting, even if we do it most of the time we talk. I think we should attempt to stop that, don't you? My nerves can't take it anymore, and I really don't want to have to start taking those anxiety medications I keep hearing about. I decided not to go to a doctor about it and try to fix the problem myself."

Destiny grinned. Her mother would self-diagnose and then self-treat. Destiny assumed it was her way of playing the part of a doctor, so she could have a little more in common with her husband.

"Anyway, I called because I wanted to tell you that I've been reading your blog each day and—"

"You read my blog?" Destiny couldn't disguise her shock. Her mother had always appeared uninterested in her magazine, her blog or anything else that didn't involve her obtaining a "real" job.

"You don't have to sound *so* surprised. But yes, I do. And for the longest time, I thought it was simply a means of passing your time, a way for you to pretend you were doing something with your life."

Destiny nodded. Now *this* was the mother she knew, and she prepared for the typical "words of wisdom" normally delivered from Geneva Porter when she was on a mission to dictate Destiny's life.

"But I was wrong."

Destiny blinked, not at all anticipating those four words from her mother. "You were?"

"Yes. In all honesty, your blogs initially were so pitiful. All of your posts about dates that had gone wrong and how there was no such thing as a true Southern gentleman. Your daddy was always a gentleman when we dated. He still is, really. It's just that you haven't gotten to spend a whole lot of time with him over the years with his work schedule and all. But in any case, in your blogs you discounted the possibility of a real gentleman, and that hurt, because I realized that you'd never gotten to see that part of your father. Maybe that even tainted your view of how men should treat a lady. And I could've helped that if I'd have told you more about his good qualities, and the way he is."

"I've never thought that Daddy wasn't great," Destiny said. But her mother was right; she hadn't seen him show a whole lot of affection toward her mother, not the way she saw other couples show affection, like the Tingles, the Tollesons, the Grahams and every other long-lasting couple she'd interviewed in Claremont. And for the first time, Destiny felt sorry for her mom.

"I know," her mother said, "but in your blogs, I got the sense that you didn't believe in something that I still believe in. Your daddy still treats me that way, even if it's only on rare occasions."

Like holidays and vacations, Destiny realized, which were the only times she ever thought her mother seemed happy.

"But then, as time has gone by, and particularly over the last month, as you've written about the Southern country boy with the big heart, and all of these wonderful love stories that you've posted in the past few weeks, I've looked forward to checking the posts each morning. And I feel like I've gotten a glimpse of your happiness, that I can see you're doing something that you love." A sniff through the line alerted Destiny to the fact that her mother had started to cry. "I'm so glad that you're able to do that, Destiny. It—it means the world to me. I can't tell you what it would've meant to me if I could've…" Her voice drifted off, and she sniffed again. "I just wanted you to know that I understand that you're happy, and I am happy for you, too."

For the first time in her life, Destiny thought she saw a glimpse of what her mother felt, and she also believed she understood. "Mom, what is it that *you* love to do? What was *your* dream?" She waited for her mother's answer while mentally kicking herself for never thinking to ask before. She'd always assumed her mother seemed miserable because she liked being miserable. Now she suspected there was more to Geneva Porter than she'd realized.

"I had a degree in photography, you know," her mother whispered.

Destiny had nearly forgotten about her mother's degree. "You wanted to be a photographer." It wasn't a question. She knew the answer. Her mother always had a camera nearby, and volunteered to take the photos at all of their family functions, as well as every school activity. And yet Destiny hadn't realized that she wasn't merely doing it to save a memento of the event. She did it because that's what she loved. "Why didn't you pursue that as a career?"

"Your father said he made plenty to support our family, and he did, of course. There was no need for me to work outside the home. And he really liked me staying at home, being here for y'all when he was working all of those crazy hours and being here for him whenever he got home from work."

"But that's your dream," Destiny said, as the pieces clicked into place. Her mother had given up her dream for her father and for Destiny and Bevvie. Then she'd tried to make sure Destiny and Bevvie made solid career choices for themselves because she'd never had the chance.

"We're not going to talk about that now," her mother said. "I mainly wanted to tell you that I've been reading your latest posts, and you have a lot of talent when it comes to sharing love stories. I think you should keep doing what you're doing, and I hope that one day you'll have a love story of your own to share."

Destiny glanced at the vase filled with flowers, thought of the guy who'd completely won her heart. "Mom, I do have a love story to share." Then she talked to her mother the way she never had, sharing the whirlwind of events that had occurred over the past few weeks and how much she adored Troy. By the time they disconnected, they'd talked for over an hour, and Destiny felt closer to her mother than she ever had before.

But more than that, she'd made a decision. Her mother had been miserable because she hadn't told the truth about her dream. She had essentially lied to all of them for years, and because of that, her relationship with Destiny—with her entire family, really—had been strained. Destiny didn't want to have hidden secrets in her relationship with Troy. But she did. And she knew what she had to do to make things right. She would have to tell him the truth about the reason she'd come to Claremont.

Chapter Ten

Destiny,
I can't tell you how amazing it is to write this
letter and to know that I'm writing it to you.
The past few weeks have been, quite honestly,
the best weeks of my life. I prayed for you before I even knew your name. I've written to you
for a decade and a half. And God has answered
those prayers.

You've captured my heart, and I look forward
to a day—soon—that I will give you these letters and ask you to be my wife. I know this has
all happened fast, but in my mind, my love for
you has been building for years. I'm ready to
begin our lives together, as one.
Yours forever,
Troy

As Troy drove to the B and B, he thought about the
fact that he'd started addressing his letters to Destiny,
and it simply felt right putting a name to the woman he
loved, the woman he planned to spend the rest of his

life with. He'd been as surprised as everyone else at how quickly he'd fallen when he finally met the right one, but fallen he had. And he didn't want to waste another minute in dating limbo. He'd been ready for marriage for years; he simply hadn't met his future bride.

Now he had.

Troy had written another letter today, the one that he would give Destiny tonight, and the one that would spark the beginning of their lives together. He glanced at the white envelope on the seat beside him and thought about everything he'd written inside: the confessions of love, the promises of faithfulness. He'd give her this letter tonight, and then he'd let her know about the other letters that he'd written to her over the years. Because Troy had no doubt, from that very first letter he wrote when he was twelve, whether they'd had her name on them or not, they were all addressed to one woman: Destiny.

He pulled into the driveway, saw her car parked out back and looked to the spot where he normally found her, the white rocker on the front porch, but it was empty. It still surprised him, the hint of disappointment he felt when he expected to see her and didn't. He didn't like thinking of her away from him in any way, shape or form. But pretty soon, if she said yes, she'd always be a part of him. "Till death do we part," he whispered, sliding his hand into his pocket and feeling the small box that held his great-grandmother's ring. As the oldest male grandchild, that ring was intended for his bride, and he'd asked his grandfather for the precious heirloom this morning. He'd known better than to ask his grandmother; she wasn't the best at keeping secrets. But he knew Jolaine Bowers would be thrilled with the news, even if she had gotten her wires crossed a few weeks ago and assumed that Haley Calhoun was "the one."

She'd laughed when Troy told her that he and Becca had been talking about Destiny, not Haley, when she'd eavesdropped on their conversation, and now that she'd spent quite a bit of time with his writer, she'd decided Troy made the perfect choice, and that he was no longer a player. According to his grandmother, she'd made sure everyone in town knew, from the beauty shop ladies to the quilting group to her online loop.

He grinned. Whether she spread the news or not, he had a pretty good idea that the whole town knew. For the past three weeks, he hadn't gone a day without spending as much time as possible with Destiny. And he only wanted to see her more.

He picked up the letter, got out of his truck and started toward the front door, but then heard Destiny call his name from behind him. Turning, he saw his future bride holding Mitch Gillespie's baby girl in Mitch's front yard across the street. Mitch, one of his fellow baseball players and a friend since high school, was in his driveway helping his two-year-old, Dee, ride a tricycle while Destiny held baby Emmie.

"Hey, buddy," Mitch called, "your girlfriend offered to hold Emmie while I help Dee stay on the bike."

The two-year-old, seeing she was included in the conversation, stopped moving the pedals completely and widened her eyes at Troy. "I falled off." She stuck out her lower lip and pointed to a scrape on her left knee.

"Aw, bless your heart." Troy neared the little girl. "You didn't want a bandage on it?"

She had two tiny red pigtails, and they bounced with the shake of her head. "No, Daddy kiss it, and Dessi kiss it, too."

"I'm Dessi, by the way." Destiny smiled, shifting her weight from hip to hip while gently bouncing Mitch's newest bundle of joy. Mitch had lost his wife to breast cancer shortly after Emmie's birth, and now he was raising a two-year-old and a six-month-old on his own. But Mitch had started to smile a little again, moving past the mourning period and learning to enjoy the two beautiful reminders of his beloved Jana. However, it wasn't Mitch's smile that Troy noticed now; it was Destiny's.

She nuzzled Emmie's crop of downy strawberry fuzz and grinned when the baby tried to gnaw on her cheek in an attempted kiss. "I think she likes me," Destiny said.

Mitch agreed. "That's a definite."

Troy watched the woman he loved hold the baby girl and imagined another baby in her arms. Their baby.

"Hungry, Daddy." Dee stretched one foot to the ground and tried to climb off the tricycle.

"Looks like playtime is turning into snack time now. Thanks for helping me out, Destiny." Mitch helped Dee off the tricycle and then walked toward Destiny and reached for Emmie. "You're a real natural," he said, then he grinned at Troy as though he knew exactly what Troy was thinking.

Troy smiled back, quietly acknowledging that he thought she was a "natural," too.

"I'm across the street if you need any help with them again," Destiny said, as Mitch started toward his house. "Anytime, really," she added.

"I appreciate that." Mitch slowed at the stairs, while Dee, playing Miss Independent, waved off his assistance and climbed them on her own, her little hands grasping the rails as she wobbled up.

Troy and Destiny watched until the trio disappeared into the house, then Destiny sighed. "They're beautiful, aren't they?"

"Yes, they are." But as beautiful as Dee and Emmie were, the woman standing next to him was even more beautiful in Troy's eyes. And tonight, he'd ask her to be his bride. He simply had to wait for the right moment.

"What's that?" she asked, eyeing the envelope he held in his hand.

Troy meant to fold it and put it in his pocket, but in his haste to see her, he'd forgotten. "It's a letter."

"Oh," she whispered.

"It's for you, but I'd planned on giving it to you later." He noted her anxious expression, like a kid who could see the presents under the tree but knew she had to wait however many days necessary until opening them at Christmas. "Here, you can hold on to it, but don't open it until I tell you to, okay?"

Her attention went to her own name, written on the outside of the envelope, and then she slowly reached for it.

"Don't worry," he said softly, "it's a good letter. I promise."

Destiny took the envelope, then looked up, a misty sheen coating her eyes. "You're sure it's for me?"

"Has your name on it, doesn't it?" he asked jokingly. The way she held the envelope, as though it were a priceless treasure, touched his heart. If she knew the depth of the words he'd written inside, or the fact that he'd written countless other letters for her, she'd realize that it was as much of a treasure as Troy had to give. His love, from now until eternity.

She again stared at the envelope. "I don't have my purse with me. Is it okay if I fold it and put it in my pocket?"

He smiled. "Sure."

She carefully folded the envelope in half and then slid it into her front pocket.

"You want to walk to the square?" He held out a hand, and she slipped hers inside, her soft, warm palm finding its place perfectly within his.

"Yes, I do."

Troy inwardly celebrated her choice of words and wondered how long he'd have to wait until he heard them again…in a church, in front of all of their family and friends.

As they walked, she leaned against him and sighed. "I love it here."

He kissed the top of her head, smiled against her silky hair and thanked God that she indeed loved it here and prayed that she would hopefully want to stay here, with him, forever. "I'm glad."

An afternoon rain shower, typical for midsummer,

had left the flowers and trees along Maple Street glistening and resulted in a soothing afternoon breeze that carried the scent of magnolias. Claremont was always beautiful, but it seemed to shine a little brighter today, creating a perfect setting for a proposal. He visualized himself on one knee by the three-tiered fountain in the square, the water's mist kissing their faces as Destiny said she'd live here forever as his wife.

He could hardly wait.

When they reached the square, however, he saw the area around the fountain filled with people, couples sitting on the wrought-iron benches feeding the geese, teens playing Frisbee and kids flying kites. He scanned for another private area where they could talk, but the place was almost as crowded as First Friday. Then again, the rain they'd had earlier had produced the type of weather for enjoying the square, so he understood everyone's reason for being here. But it sure blew the intimate setting he'd planned out of the water.

He considered suggesting they go back to the B and B and then drive to Hydrangea Park. One of the white gazebos at the park would make a nice location for a proposal, or even the botanical garden area beside the heart-shaped pond. But he knew several baseball teams played out there during the week, and undoubtedly people who didn't find their way to the square on this beautiful day would probably find their way to the park.

"Troy," Destiny said, as they neared the Sweet Stop.

He'd been so wrapped up in trying to figure out where he could propose that he hadn't said a word while they walked to the square. "Yes?"

"I—I need to talk to you about something, tell you something." The worry in her voice bothered him, and he wondered if she was thinking about going back to Atlanta. He didn't want her to even consider it, if she would be willing to live here from now on. From the way Troy saw it, she could write anywhere, especially since she was her own boss. He'd even noticed the *Claremont News* looking for a reporter and had planned to suggest she apply for that job, if she thought she had to have a regular nine-to-five type position. But Troy didn't see a real reason for that. If she wanted to keep pursuing her dream of becoming published, she could. He didn't make a ton of money, but he made enough, and he'd support her completely if she wanted to go for her dream, or if she simply wanted to stay home and raise their children.

He couldn't wait to have children with Destiny.

"Troy?" she repeated, and he realized he hadn't answered.

"You can talk to me about anything," he said, "always. But before you tell me whatever you've got to tell me, I've got something I want to talk to you about first. It's just that I'm thinking I want to—discuss it somewhere else." The sidewalk in front of the candy store, where an abundance of people were sitting around eating ice cream, wasn't exactly what he had planned for the place he asked her to be his wife.

"O-kay," she said, but her upper teeth grazed her lower lip, and she couldn't disguise her worry.

He figured this had to do with her leaving Claremont, but he also assumed that her apprehension would disappear when she learned he wanted to get married and that he didn't want to wait. Then she could simply stay here. He'd marry her tomorrow if she'd be okay with that. "We'll talk before the night's over," he promised, "but I want to wait until we can have a little more privacy, okay?"

"Okay." She seemed a little more at ease as they moved toward his grandparents' store.

The front door of Bowers' Sporting Goods swung open as they neared, and Troy's grandmother hopped out to greet them.

"Hey! I thought that was you I saw through the crowd. This pretty day has everyone out and shopping. Isn't it great? Don't you just love it here, Destiny?" Ever since she'd realized that Destiny was more than a one-date kind of girl for Troy, she'd laid on the Clare-mont talk rather thick, but Troy didn't mind. He'd been doing the same thing.

"I do love it here," Destiny said, but for some reason, Troy thought he heard another hint of sadness in her tone, probably because she didn't want to leave. But he was glad for that. He wanted her to stay, too.

"That's great," his grandmother said. "And I'm glad I spotted y'all. David Presley is having a sidewalk sale at A Likely Story. I thought we could walk over and check out all of the great deals on the books, and while we're there we can talk to him about promoting your novels one day."

Troy grinned. Destiny had attempted to tell his grandmother several times over the past few weeks that she hadn't actually written a novel yet, but that didn't stop Jolaine Bowers from trying to promote the future—and as of yet nonexistent—books. Destiny seemed to understand that it made his grandmother feel good to help, and she didn't repeat the fact that there were no novels to sell.

"I'd love to meet him. I've seen him at church a few times, but I haven't had a chance to talk to him yet."

"Wonderful. You can talk to him now." Troy's grandmother yanked the door open to their store and yelled in, "James, I'll be back in a little bit. I'm going to introduce Destiny to David Presley!" She waited for his response telling them to have fun and then shut the door. "Okay, we're all set." She clapped her hands together and led the way, weaving through the crowd as they progressed along the sidewalk toward the bookstore.

A huge white sign with Sidewalk Sale in bright blue letters covered the brick wall beside the bookstore. Assorted shelves on rollers filled the sidewalk in front of the place, and Claremont shoppers were everywhere. The majority of the books were used, with the prices on the sale racks ranging anywhere from a quarter to a dollar. Troy wasn't sure how David Presley made a living from the place he'd inherited from his grandmother, but he always had a smile for his customers and seemed to be doing okay.

"Here you go, Zeb." David handed a plastic bag filled with books to one of the oldest men in the county, Zeb Shackleford.

Zeb took the bag and attempted to give David a few dollars, but the bookstore owner shook his head. "No, sir. I know you let the shut-ins and the nursing home patients keep the books after you read to them.

There's no way I'm gonna charge you. Your smile is payment enough for me."

Troy grinned, falling more and more in love with Claremont and the people that lived here each day. It seemed he was always learning something new, and positive, about his neighbors. Now was no exception. He was glad Destiny also seemed fixated on the conversation between the two men.

"That David, he's a nice young man, isn't he?" Troy's grandmother had obviously also witnessed David's gift to old Zeb.

"Yes, he is," Troy agreed. "And I bet he'll be happy to promote Destiny's books one day."

"I know!" She giddily clapped her hands together while Destiny shook her head at Troy.

"You're terrible, getting her hopes up like that," she whispered.

"Who says you won't have a book in his store one day? I'm simply preparing the way for when you do." He squeezed her hand and liked the way her eyes lit up at the mention of her publishing a novel. As much as she claimed she didn't have one in the works, he'd suspected from their talks over the weeks that her bucket list included penning a book. He'd already started praying that her dream would become a reality; not just that dream but all of her dreams.

Troy's grandmother waited for David and Zeb to finish talking, then she tapped the bookstore owner's shoulder. "David, I want to introduce you to Destiny Porter."

He turned and extended a hand. "Hello, Destiny. I

believe I've seen you at church with Troy. It's nice to finally meet you."

"You, too," she said, shaking his hand.

"How've things been going, Troy?" he asked, but before Troy could answer, his grandmother jumped back in.

"Destiny is a writer from Atlanta. She's probably going to have a book you can sell here someday, and so I told her you'd let her have a book signing here when she's ready."

"I am a writer, but I haven't actually written a full-length book yet. I write articles, mostly," Destiny explained.

David grinned. "Well, when you get a book ready, I'll be glad to set up a signing." He released her hand and squinted at her for a moment. "Did you say your last name is Porter?"

Destiny nodded. "Yes. Do you know some Porters?"

"No, but…" His eyes widened. "Wait a minute. You're Destiny Porter, from Atlanta. I remember now why your name sounded familiar. You started that online magazine, *Southern Love,* right?" His smile stretched and he nodded. "Yes, that's it. You've really got a knack at writing. I've especially enjoyed the love-letter segment. Looking forward to when you reveal the winner's letters next week. I advertised the contest in my store, but I don't suppose anyone from Claremont entered."

Troy and Destiny had discussed her digital magazine a few times over the past few weeks, and she'd told him in detail about the blog entries she'd put out while she'd been in town, the ones about couples from Claremont. But he hadn't heard anything about a love-letter segment, or the fact that she'd had some type of contest. Why wouldn't she have mentioned that, too, if it was as big of a deal as David seemed to think?

"I'm glad you like it," she said softly, her eyes fixed on David and refusing to look at Troy.

"That's your magazine?" Troy's grandmother's surprise seemed even more intense than David's had been. "So you're the one I sent those letters to?"

Destiny's mouth flattened, her eyes watered, and a flush of red crept up her cheeks. "They actually went to my managing editor, but I did see them," she admitted, her voice so quiet Troy could barely hear.

But he did hear, and he wanted some answers. However, his grandmother wasn't finished yet.

"She told me that you wouldn't print them. She mailed them back to me, and I already put them back—" her eyes darted to Troy "—back where they belong. She *promised* you wouldn't print them. You don't have his permission, so you can't. That's what she said."

"Whose permission?" Troy asked, his voice as raspy and raw as his insides felt right now, because the pieces were falling into place, and he didn't like where they were landing at all. His mind recalled that day he'd found his grandmother going through the boxes in his garage. "What letters did you send in?" He tried to control the anger making his words snap, but he could tell by the way his grandmother's lip trembled that she'd done…exactly what he feared.

"They promised they wouldn't publish them," she whispered.

"And we didn't," Destiny said, finally looking at Troy while tears filled her eyes. "We didn't have your permission, so we couldn't publish them."

"I sent your letters in, Troy. Just a few of them, because I knew no one had written love letters the way you had, and I thought they'd probably win the contest. The winner gets a thousand dollars, and I was going to give you the money, but I didn't think about needing your permission if I won. And then I realized that you wouldn't have wanted me sending them, because they're private. I don't know what I was thinking." Her head shook and her voice trembled. "I was wrong, and so I asked to get them back. And I did get them back and put them where I found them."

"Troy's the one you've been talking about in your blog?" David questioned, then snapped his mouth shut when Destiny gasped.

"You've been blogging about me?" He didn't attempt to disguise his anger now, and the crowd shopping around them all stopped to see the show. Destiny had been telling him about her blog because they both knew he wasn't a "surfing the web" kind of guy. He hadn't taken the time to search out her blog because he'd assumed she told him what was in it. All of those discussions about the stories she'd written each day, and none of them even hinted that she was also writing about Troy. "Since when, Destiny? And tell me something—when were you going to tell me that you'd read those letters? Or that you planned on printing them—" he remembered David's words "—next week?"

"I wasn't going to." She shook her head. "I promise. I still didn't know what I was going to put in the issue, but I wasn't going to print the letters. Believe me, Troy, we really did mail them back."

"We? Just how many people have seen them?" Troy's pulse pounded so hard his temples throbbed.

"Only me and Rita," Destiny whispered, her tears spilling freely over her cheeks. "I was going to tell you, Troy, tonight. I was. That's what I wanted to talk to you—"

He held up a hand. "You said you came to Claremont to write about small-town living." His head shook as every horrible piece fell into place and he remembered that very first day that she drove into town…and started her trip at the service station where he worked. "That wasn't true, was it? You didn't come here to write about Claremont. You came here to write about me. You came here so you could print my letters. My *private* letters. All of this time, since that first day, has been a lie."

"Troy, wait, I need to explain…"

"You think I'd believe anything you say now? Really?" He thought of what he'd planned to talk to her about tonight and how very wrong he'd been. "I don't want to see you again, Destiny."

She reached for him, but he shook her arm away.

"Don't even think of printing those letters, not one word of them. They're meant for someone." He inhaled, released it thickly. "Someone special."

"Troy, I promise you, I wasn't going to—"

But he didn't hear the rest of her plea. He turned and stormed away from the bookstore, away from the crowd that stared at him with pity, away from his guilt-ridden grandmother and away from the only woman who'd ever hurt him…and the only one he'd ever truly loved.

Chapter Eleven

"Destiny, you know you can stay here as long as you want. Your daddy and I are really enjoying having you back at home, and I know Bevvie likes it." Geneva Porter lifted the newspaper classifieds and pointed to the rental properties Destiny had highlighted. "There's no need for you to move out. Why don't you stay here until you figure out what you want to do?"

Destiny finished the letter she'd been writing and folded it to keep her mother from seeing the contents. "Mom, I wouldn't have moved in now, but I couldn't afford the rent in that fancy Buckhead apartment. I don't know why I picked something like that fresh out of college anyway."

"You were counting on your magazine doing well because you believed in it," her mother said. "There's nothing wrong with that."

Destiny liked this new positive side of Geneva Porter, but unfortunately, she couldn't reciprocate the optimism. "Well, I pegged that wrong, didn't I?"

Her mother sat on the edge of Destiny's bed. "You

still have subscribers. Rita said you'd lost some, but not all."

"Subscribers are good, but it's the advertisers who pay the bills. And they all left when I didn't deliver an issue last month." She added the folded letter to the box that held all of the others. "And Rita said she's sure I'll get that hostess job at the restaurant where she works. That'll give me enough to live on until I can find some kind of real writing job."

"You have a real writing job, honey." Her mother glanced at the box of letters, but Destiny wasn't worried. She knew her mother would never read her private letters, unlike Destiny, who'd read Troy's until she could recite every word.

A whimper escaped, and she attempted to swallow it down before her mother started feeling sorry for her again. Then she caught her mom's look of pity and knew she'd heard.

"I'll be okay," she said, for the thousandth time since she'd moved home a month ago.

Her mother smoothed her hand across the white comforter on Destiny's bed. "Troy's grandmother called me today."

That got Destiny's attention. "Mrs. Bowers? How'd she get your number?"

"She said Rita gave it to her."

Destiny made a mental note to alert her sole employee as to what personal information she was allowed to share. "What did she say?" She tried not to sound too eager to hear the answer and failed miserably.

"She said that Troy hasn't been the same since you

left town, that he's miserable and that she thinks you should come back so y'all can work things out." Geneva cleared her throat. "I told her you were undoubtedly more miserable, and that I also think you should go back and try to work things out."

"He hasn't called, hasn't emailed, hasn't texted. He doesn't want to communicate with me, doesn't ever want to see me again," Destiny said. "His words."

Her mother lifted a shoulder. "He was hurt, honey. People say things they don't mean when they're hurt. You should go down there and see if you can fix this."

"I can't."

"Can't? Or won't?"

"Both." Destiny reached for her notepad and prepared to pen yet another letter. The letters were her only solace now, and she simply couldn't stop writing them.

Her mother looked at the notepad and then to the box filled with letters. "Rita said that you still have subscribers."

"I know. She tells me daily. But if we don't have any material worthy of advertisers, it doesn't really matter whether people subscribe, does it? And I'm kind of surprised they still subscribe anyway. I haven't put anything up since I told them I didn't get permission to run the love letters."

"Right, I was just thinking…" She touched a finger to the box of letters. "You don't have Troy's love letters anymore, but you do still have original letters you could publish."

"Trust me, Mom. Those aren't love letters. They're sad letters, depressed letters, aching-for-love letters."

Her mother nodded and touched the top of the box of letters again. "Still, I wonder if people—and one person in particular—wouldn't be interested in reading them." She rubbed her palm across the top letter. "And you wouldn't have to worry about getting the author's permission, now would you?"

Destiny processed what her mother was saying and thought about putting her innermost feelings, her raw pain and heartache, out for the world to see. The thought terrified her, and yet...that was what she'd originally planned to do to Troy, put his innermost secrets out for the world to see. "Mom?"

"Yes?"

Destiny grabbed her laptop from the nightstand and then lifted the box of letters and placed them beside her on the bed. "Thanks." She had some typing to do.

Troy cranked the engine on Chad Martin's car and was almost disappointed it sounded so good. The old BMW was the last vehicle in for repair, and Troy didn't want any idle time on his hands. Ever since Destiny left, he'd worked from sunup until sundown at the station during the week, then at the fishing hole on the weekends, to keep himself as busy as possible and to keep his mind off the stunning brunette who'd broken his heart.

Probably because he'd been working so much, he'd finished every single job. Frowning, he turned the key and realized that, like it or not, he had the car running again. He ran a hand over the dash of the older-model car and instantly remembered the newer model, shiny and red, pulling into the station that first time with

Destiny sitting behind the wheel. What a whirlwind his life had been since that day. And how much it had changed. Before, nearly every day he at least thought about writing a letter to his future bride. Now the thought of writing one, the thought of even *having* a future bride, was as foreign as this car.

"Troy, you in there?" Bo Taylor's voice called into the shop.

Troy swallowed past the realization that he might want to stay single for life, climbed out of the car and slammed the door with enough force to make the windows rattle. "Aw, man, I didn't mean to do that. Had my mind on something else."

Bo nodded as though he knew exactly where Troy's mind had been. "That car has enough miles on it that I'm sure it's been through harder blows than that, and it doesn't seem any worse for the wear."

"Still." Troy sighed and didn't add anything else. What could he say? His heart was hurting, and because of it, he wanted to hurt something. Even so, he should hurt something he owned instead of something that belonged to a customer.

"Well, um, the reason I came out here is because you've got someone here to see you."

Troy had been secretly waiting for this for weeks. His grandmother had hinted that she'd asked Destiny to come back and work things out, and he'd wondered what he'd say when she showed up. He still didn't know. He'd been hurt terribly, but he still loved her terribly.

"Who's here?" he asked, then held his breath and

waited to finally see her again, walking into his shop and telling him she wanted to work things out.

"David, you can come on in," Bo said, then he left the garage as David Presley stepped around the corner.

All of Troy's anticipation faded in one fell swoop. It wasn't Destiny at all, and the disappointment that washed over him made him feel even worse. He'd blown up at her, told her never to come back and that he didn't want to see her again, and she was giving him what he wanted. He should be happy. And he shouldn't take this disappointment out on David the way he'd taken his anger out on Chad's car. He inhaled, let it out and welcomed the guy.

"Hey, David. Got troubles with your vehicle?" Maybe he'd be able to stay busy a few more hours today, after all.

The bookstore owner shook his head. "No, the old Mustang is running fine, even if it should be on its last leg," David said. "But I came because I wanted to give you something."

Troy hadn't noticed the box tucked under David's right arm. "Give me something?"

"Listen, I've felt horrible since that night when I told you about Destiny's contest. Seeing her get so upset and seeing you get so angry, all because of something I said, well, that's kind of tough to stomach, you know?"

"It wasn't your fault, David. She should've told me about the love-letter contest." He grabbed a shop rag out of his back pocket and wiped his hands. "Nothing you should feel bad about, and you sure don't need to give me any kind of a gift."

"You know, she said she was going to tell you about the contest that night, and she also said she'd decided not to print the letters," David reminded him.

Troy nodded. He remembered her words clearly. "Yeah, but she also told me she was a writer from Atlanta, yet never once mentioned that she came here to write about me."

David held out the box. "I don't suppose you've been following her blog, or looked at the new issue of her magazine she put out this week?"

Troy had fought the urge to look at her site, and thankfully, because he'd been so busy working, he'd succeeded in resisting the temptation. "No, I haven't."

David nodded. "I figured as much, so I printed these out for you. She's been posting the love letters for the past week, and I thought you'd want to see them."

Troy couldn't believe it. Destiny had said she'd mailed the letters back, and his grandmother had promised she received them and put them back in their corresponding boxes in his garage. And there were no new letters because Troy hadn't been able to write another one to his future bride since the bride he thought he wanted left town.

"She made copies?" Anger ripped through him at a feverish pace. He reached in his pocket, pulled out his phone and prepared to dial the woman he hadn't spoken to in over a month…and give her a piece of his mind. "She had no right to publish my letters."

"They aren't your letters." David extended the box.

Confused, Troy reminded the guy, "I wrote them."

"No, you didn't." He lifted the top of the box so Troy could see the stack of typed letters, and he easily spotted the salutation that began the first page.

My dearest Troy.

"She published *her* love letters," David said, "the ones she wrote to you. And she's put them out for the whole world to see."

"She put up love letters…addressed to me?" Troy couldn't believe what he was hearing. "How many love letters?

"So far a hundred and two. I've printed them all out for you." He handed Troy the box.

Troy lifted the pages, flipped through them to see each covered with text, love letters addressed to him. A hundred and two letters? On Destiny's website? He swallowed past the thickness in his throat and looked up at David. "Thank you."

"You're welcome. And just so you know, I think she means every word."

"We do, too," Maura said, as she and Bo stepped around the corner. They'd obviously been eavesdropping, but Troy didn't care. He only wanted to read the letters.

Fishing his keys out of his pocket, he started toward his truck with the box of letters. "Bo, will you call Chad and tell him his car is ready? I'm going home." Then he looked again to David. "And thank you for this." He held up the box.

David nodded. "Let me know what happens. I'll be praying for you, for both of you."

"We will, too," Maura promised.

Troy left and immediately felt the power of knowing

people were indeed praying for him and for Destiny. And he wondered what she'd said in those letters…and what he'd do when he finished reading them.

Chapter Twelve

"I can't believe how fast everything has turned around, can you? I mean, our subscribers have quadrupled in the past week, and they're climbing by the minute!" Rita practically cheered the news through the line. "And Lamont Sharp wanting to publish your book? Isn't this incredible? You're going to have a successful online magazine *and* a book published in print, too! Isn't that great?"

"Yes, it is." Destiny couldn't muster the excitement her friend had about the response from her love letters. Yes, their magazine was thriving, but that didn't help Destiny's heart or the sadness when she thought about what she'd lost. She sat on her parents' back porch, stared out at the pool and the manicured gardens, and wished she was back on the front porch of the Claremont Bed and Breakfast. She was glad she'd mended fences with her mom, but she missed visiting with the Tingles and the Tollesons. She missed helping Mitch Gillespie with his little girls. She missed Claremont, period. And more than that, she missed Troy.

But he hadn't called, hadn't even responded to all of the letters she'd posted begging his forgiveness and proclaiming her love…and the fact that she was certain she'd never love anyone else that way again.

"Destiny? Are you even listening to me? I asked what city you plan to visit first for your love stories."

She blinked back tears. How was she going to write about love stories when she'd ruined the only love story that mattered…her own? "I can't talk right now, Rita. I'll call you later."

"Okay, but are you going to post another letter today? The subscribers are loving them, you know. Our numbers go up every time you put one out."

Destiny already had her computer on her lap. "Yes, I'm about to write one now."

"Awesome. Okay, call me back later."

"I will," she promised, then disconnected and logged on to her site. The love letters had become almost as therapeutic as her new prayer life, giving her a means to share her feelings with the world and helping her magazine in the process. In her dreams, Troy read each letter she posted; in reality, she suspected he didn't even know her site address and hadn't bothered trying to find it.

But that didn't matter. He'd written his love letters for years without even knowing the recipient. She'd write hers, too, but each of hers weren't addressed to her future husband. Instead, they were addressed to the one she'd never have because of her lies.

Sniffing, she put her fingers to the keys and began yet another letter to the man she loved.

Dear Troy,

Today is Sunday, and I went to church this morning. Before I met you, I went occasionally, but I didn't feel that compulsion to go, to worship God and talk to Him and grow closer to Him, the way you are close to Him. I honestly don't know what I'd do now if I didn't have my faith. It gets me through the sad days, the days I find myself in tears over what might have been. I hope that one day you can forgive me for deceiving you. I hope that one day I can forgive myself. Because by lying to you, I deprived myself of the thing I want more than anything... true love. And I know our love would have been even stronger because we'd have had God in the center, the way you described when you first showed me that verse in Ecclesiastes 4:12, the one that explained how a cord of three strands isn't easily broken.

The thing is, I've found the love of God that you wanted in your future bride. I love Him so much, and I love Him even more, I think, because you brought me to Him. I wish I could tell you all of this in person because it means so much to me now. But I suspect you don't read my blog, and you probably haven't read any of these letters. Even so, I will write to you and pray that you will find the woman you deserve, find the one who you've written to for a decade and a half. Any woman would be blessed to be on the receiving end of your love. I felt it for the briefest of times and yet I'll hold on to that memory, the memory of being loved by you, for the rest of my life.

I love you, Troy Lee. Forever and always,

Destiny

She posted the letter, then closed her eyes and leaned her head back on the rocker. So many letters and none of them reaching the recipient, oddly familiar to Troy's letters intended for his bride. "Oh, Troy," she whispered, "I love you so."

Her phone rang again, and she glanced at the display then answered. "Hey, Mom."

"Hey, honey. You doing okay?"

"Yeah, I'm okay." Destiny's dad had been off this morning and the entire family went to church together. It'd been nice sitting on the pew with her parents, Bevvie and Jared at their large church in Atlanta, but it had only reminded her of how much she'd enjoyed the small community church in Claremont and the way each member knew everyone else. The people in Atlanta were friendly, but she only knew the families who sat in front of and behind them.

She had skipped going out to lunch with her parents because she simply wanted to get away from crowds of people she didn't know and get back home.

"We met a guy at lunch today, and we've asked him to come back to the house and visit for a while. Is that okay with you?" her mother continued.

Destiny frowned. They were bringing some guy they just met home? "You're bringing someone here?" She'd come home because she didn't want to hang around a bunch of strangers all afternoon and now they were bringing one? "Mom, I'll probably go up to my room. I'm not really feeling all that up to visiting."

"You sure about that?"

Destiny recognized that beautiful deep drawl and dropped the phone when she saw Troy standing on the back porch with her parents.

Her hand flew to her mouth and she mumbled, "Troy?"

"This is the guy we met at lunch." Her mother dropped her cell phone into her purse. "Actually, he called and asked us to meet him there, and we had a very enjoyable visit, wouldn't you say, Phillip?"

Destiny's father patted Troy's shoulder and nodded. "Very enjoyable, Geneva. But I have a feeling he wants to visit with Destiny now, and we should probably head on in." He turned to Troy. "Nice to meet you, son. And I mean that."

"You, too, sir." Troy smiled but barely glanced at Destiny's parents as they disappeared into the house; his attention was as focused on her as hers was on him.

"You had lunch with my parents?" she asked, her mind reeling from the realization that he'd not only met her parents but that he was here, in Atlanta, on her porch. And talking to her. *Please, please, God. Let him forgive me. Give me another chance with Troy.*

He slowly moved toward her, and Destiny fought the urge to jump up from the rocker and into his arms. She didn't know yet if he wanted her again, but she hoped and prayed that he did. "I needed to talk to them about a few things," he said.

"They knew you were coming?" She couldn't imagine how her mother would have been able to keep that from her. She could have at least encouraged her to fix up a little. Destiny had changed out of her church dress into an old T-shirt and ragged shorts.

He shook his head. "No, I called them when I was almost here and asked if they could meet me somewhere. They said they'd just left the church and suggested we have lunch. And then we had a nice visit."

"A nice visit," Destiny repeated, wondering what they'd visited about.

Troy moved directly in front of her rocker, sat on the railing and faced her. "Yes, a nice visit. And I want to tell you about it, but first I need to ask you something."

She moistened her lips, prepared for whatever he would ask, and said a quick prayer that she'd answer correctly. "Okay."

"Those letters you've been writing…"

She nodded. "Yes?"

"Did you mean what you said in them, or were you just trying to boost your subscribers?"

A sharp pang pierced her heart that he would even insinuate that she had merely been pulling a publicity stunt, but then again, her track record with him wasn't so good. She'd have to show him that she wasn't that girl anymore, and she wanted to start convincing him right here, right now. "I meant every word, Troy. I promise. And I hope—and I pray—that you believe me."

He moved his head in a single nod but didn't say anything for a moment, and Destiny feared he didn't believe her at all.

"I mean it," she whispered. "I do love you, Troy. I

made a horrible mistake by not telling you why I was in Claremont. And I've had to think about that and live with it every day since you told me to leave. It's been killing me because I came so close to having it, the kind of love that Marvin and Mae have, and the Tingles, and—and even my parents. The kind of love that Bevvie has found with Jared. I want that so much, but I don't want it with anyone else. I don't think I can even have it with anyone else, because—because—" her eyes filled with tears, her throat closed in, her heart ached in her chest "—my heart—belongs to—"

He leaned forward and touched his finger to her lips, then eased to his knees in front of her, those blue eyes studying her as her tears fell. "That last letter I gave you, on the night I told you to leave," he said. "Do you still have it?"

She blinked, more tears trickling down her cheeks with the action. Then she sniffed, reached into the pocket of her shorts and withdrew the folded envelope with her name written on the outside. "I carry it with me everywhere," she whispered.

Troy took the envelope, his fingers grazing hers in the process. Destiny longed to feel her hand in his again, but he hadn't reached for her hand. He'd taken the envelope and turned it over. "You never opened it."

She shook her head. "No, I didn't."

"Why not, Destiny?" He was so close now that she literally felt her heart pulling toward him, but he'd asked her a question, and she needed to answer. She never wanted to leave him wondering about anything again.

"Because it wouldn't have been right. You never

told me to open it. You said I'd open it later that night, that you'd tell me when, but we never got to that moment. And I couldn't read it without you saying it was okay."

"You read the other ones," he said, his voice soft and low but filled with emotion.

"And I'm sorry for that. But I—I think I started falling in love with you when I read those other letters." Her mouth moved into a smile. "And I'll never be sorry for that, Troy." She looked back at the letter he now held in his hands. "I couldn't read this one, though, because it was different. Special," she added. "I guess because it was written specifically to me."

"This one is special," he said, running a finger across her name on the envelope, then handing it back to Destiny. "Open it."

A rush of adrenaline caused her skin to tingle. "Are you sure?"

He nodded. "I'm sure. Open it, and read it out loud."

She turned the envelope and, with her hands trembling, pushed her finger beneath the seal to break the precious letter free. Then she withdrew the paper, slowly unfolded it and read.

Dear Destiny,

I began writing to you fifteen years ago, even though I didn't know your name. I've waited a long time, prayed a long time, for God to bring you into my life. You see, I've searched for years for the woman that I believed made my life complete, the one who I could not only share my love with, but also my faith. From the moment you entered my world, that first day when I met you at the filling station, I felt something pulling me toward you.

Sure, in the beginning, I know it was the attraction that any guy feels when he first meets a beautiful girl. But the more I've been around you, the more I've gotten to know you, the more I've realized that there was more to this feeling. It goes beyond infatuation, way beyond, and into the type of desire that I've wanted to find, not only a physical desire but a spiritual desire, as well. I have no doubt that God planned me for you, and you for me. I want to be with you always, to love you and take care of you and be a part of you, through the good and the bad. I want to truly be that cord of three that cannot be broken, you and me, with God in the center, making us strong enough to last through the bad times and strong enough to soar through the good times.

I love you, Destiny. I love you today, I'll love you tomorrow, and I'll love you to eternity. I've been waiting fifteen years to find my future bride, and now I have…if you'll say yes.

Destiny held the paper out so her tears wouldn't mar the precious words. "Are you…?" she whispered. "Do you still…?" She looked up to find him kneeling in front of her.

He gently took the letter and placed it on the porch, then he took her hands in his. "I was going to ask you that night, and then—then I let my anger get the best of me. I told myself I could ignore the feelings, that I would get past the sensation that I'd met my future bride and that my heart would eventually stop aching for you." He shook his head. "But it hasn't, and I've hated every moment I've spent away from you."

"I've hated it, too," she said, her voice quaking. "I'm so sorry I didn't tell you about the letters…."

He shook his head. "Then I read your letters to me, and I knew that you were hurting the same way, and that you had loved me the same way I loved you." A soft smile played on his mouth. "And that was an answered prayer for me, Destiny. Because I couldn't forgive myself for letting the best thing in my life slip away. And I want to ask you to forgive me. You tried to tell me the truth that night, that you'd planned to tell me about the letters, and I didn't believe you. But I do now, and I always will." He reached into his pocket and withdrew a small box.

Destiny gasped, focused on the box as he opened it and she viewed an elegant antique wedding ring. "Oh, Troy."

"This was my great-grandmother's ring," he said. "I'd planned to ask you if you'd wear it that night, but this actually worked out better because this gave me a chance to meet your family." He looked up. "And ask your father for your hand." Troy tilted his head toward the windows behind Destiny, and she turned to see her parents watching them, her father's arm around her mother and her mother's tears dripping as she smiled. Troy cleared his throat, and Destiny turned back to the man she loved. "So now it's up to you. I've searched for you for fifteen years, and I plan to love you for eternity, if you'll have me. Marry me, Destiny, and make me the happiest man in the world."

She fell off the chair and into his arms. "Oh, yes! Yes, yes, yes, I'll marry you!" She kissed his forehead, then the bridge of his nose and then finally, pressed her lips to his in the most amazing, most touching kiss she'd ever experienced. Because she was saying yes—yes!—to marry the man she loved.

When the kiss ended, she heard the back door creak open and then the sound of her parents laughing and clapping and congratulating the newly engaged couple. Destiny looked down at the ring, still in the box. In all of her celebration, she'd forgotten to give him a chance to slide it on her finger. "Please, put it on, Troy. And then I'll never, ever take it off."

Grinning, he slid the ring on her finger. "How soon can we get married?" he asked.

Destiny looked at the ring, looked at her fiancé and knew she didn't want to wait any longer either. "Is Saturday soon enough?"

She heard her mother's gasp, followed by her father's laugh and then ultimately Troy's triumphant cheer.

"Saturday," he said, "is perfect!"

Epilogue

Troy couldn't believe how excited the entire town of Claremont became for his wedding, especially the fact that they only had six days to prepare for the event. It was as though every shop owner, every church member, every family member and friend got in on the act of decorating the place for the wedding of the century, or at least of the decade.

"We've been waiting for this for years," his grandmother proclaimed several times throughout the week, and almost every time she said it, whoever happened to be within earshot responded the same: "I know, right?"

Troy attempted to help out wherever he could, but the majority of the week found him accepting hugs and high fives of congratulations or planning for their honeymoon, which they decided would be spent driving around the Southeast in search of towns for Destiny to write about in her upcoming books. Troy was so proud of his future bride and the fact that her new writing contract would provide them with a reason to travel a little and also allow her to spend the majority of her time working from home, their home, in Claremont.

Her family and her friend Rita had made a couple of trips from Atlanta this week to bring all of Destiny's things and to add a bit of a feminine touch to his place. Destiny had immediately fallen in love with the 1920s house he'd inherited from his great-grandparents. Similar to the Tingles' place, it had a porch surrounding the home and plenty of space to be filled with their love. Troy had been thrilled to hear her parents marveling at the appeal of his old house.

"A perfect location for Destiny to write," they repeated when they first looked at the place. Troy thought the same thing.

His grandmother and mother had promised that the refrigerator and freezer would be stocked when they returned from their honeymoon, with his grandma specifying she didn't want Destiny worrying about cooking when she had a book to write. Troy suspected that, if Grandma had her way, Destiny wouldn't have to cook for at least a year.

Troy loved that his family embraced his new love and had all gotten in on the fast-paced planning of the week. When Destiny said she wanted to get married by the fountain in the square, his grandfather had been the one to call a town meeting and assign duties for the special day. And the wedding decorations put the Fourth of July and First Friday scenes to shame. All the shop owners had white tulle and bows draped across their awnings. Multicolored flowers bordered the sidewalk all the way around the square and formed a path for the bride to walk from Gina Brown's Art

Gallery to the fountain. There were no chairs for guests because everyone in town had been invited, and they'd never find that many chairs to cover the square in Claremont. So the crowd stood surrounding the fountain and waiting for the appearance of Claremont's newest resident...and Troy's future bride.

"You nervous?" Aidan stood a few feet away from Troy as best man, with his three younger brothers, Josh, Adam and Cole, on the other side as groomsmen.

"Nope, just ready." And he was. He'd been preparing for this day, for this moment, since he wrote that first love letter at age twelve.

"Looks like she's ready, too," Brother Henry said, and Troy turned to see his bride. Her sister, Bevvie, along with Becca, Rita and another of Destiny's friends from college, walked ahead of her as bridesmaids, but Troy barely noticed. Destiny outshone them all.

She'd been excited about wearing her mother's wedding gown, and Troy could see why. The white lace dress fit her beautifully, showcasing her slim figure and her hair, which was falling past her shoulders the way Troy liked. But the gown had nothing on the woman wearing it. Her smile beamed as she made her way down the aisle; her eyes sparkled with excitement, with happiness. She looked...the way Troy felt.

By the time she reached the fountain and her father placed her hand in Troy's, Troy couldn't wait any longer, and he moved toward her, then brushed a tender kiss across her lips. "You're beautiful, you know, and I'm one lucky guy."

The crowd laughed, and Brother Henry shook his head.

"Troy, you do realize that goes at the end of the ceremony," the preacher said.

"Don't worry, I don't mind repeating," Troy answered and heard more giggles, including Destiny's.

Brother Henry laughed, too, then started the ceremony. Troy and Destiny said their vows flawlessly, and then they were treated to cheers and applause before the entire town joined in the reception. The Tollesons had prepared everything on their menu for the guests, and the Sweet Stop had prepared not only a wedding cake but every other kind of treat from the shop, as well as an ice-cream buffet with all of the toppings.

By the time the reception ended, everyone in town had personally congratulated the couple, and Troy was eager to leave and start the honeymoon. "Are you ready for the bombing of the birdseed?" he asked his bride.

Destiny hadn't stopped smiling since Brother Henry pronounced them husband and wife. "I am," she said, "but I need to tell my mother the news first."

"You haven't told her yet?

She grinned. "No, I was waiting for the right moment. I think that's now."

They walked to where her parents stood holding pouches of birdseed along with everyone else in town, forming the two lines leading the way to their car.

"Mom, I need to ask you something," Destiny said.

Her mother looked surprised but said, "Okay, honey, what is it?"

"I'm going to need a photographer to take pictures of the couples in my book, and Lamont Sharp said I can select the person I believe would do the best job.

You think you'd be up to it? It'd mean traveling around the South every now and then to take the pictures. But Troy and I were thinking maybe we could all do that together, make it like a family vacation." She looked to her father. "And it'd mean a lot to me, Daddy, if you'd come, too."

Her mother's eyes welled with tears, and she looked at her husband. "What do you think, Phillip? It sounds wonderful, doesn't it? It'd—it'd be a dream come true for me. Do you think you could take some days off every now and then for us to spend time together like that, as a family? Oh, Destiny, are you sure you want *me* to take the photos?"

"I can't imagine anyone I'd rather have."

"And I'm due for some time off," her father answered, causing Destiny to grab him in a fierce hug.

"Thank you, Daddy," she said. "It'll be wonderful, I just know it."

Troy hugged Destiny's mother and then shook hands with her father before turning to his bride. "So *now* are you ready for the birdseed run?"

Destiny laughed. "I am!" And then the two darted through the center of their friends and family, everyone cheering and tossing birdseed as they sprinted toward the car.

Destiny laughed breathlessly as she shut the door and additional bouts of birdseed pelted the windows. "This—this is almost too much fun to leave, isn't it?"

"Almost, but still, I'm ready to go."

"Me, too." She leaned over and kissed him, not a little peck but a long, drawn-out kiss that caused another round of cheers from the crowd. "You know," she said, when they finally ended the kiss, "if we're going to have those six kids you wrote about in your letters, we should probably start with a honeymoon baby. What do you think?"

"I think," he said, kissing her one more time because he simply couldn't help himself, "that my prayers—and every one of my letters—have been answered."

* * * * *

Dear Reader,

I saved the very first love letter my husband, J.R., wrote to me in college. Every now and then, I pull it out just to remember that feeling of getting that first love letter from the man that I believed (even that early in our relationship) was the one I'd marry and love for the rest of my life.

Troy and Destiny had to make it over some hurdles to find their way to true love. Thankfully, they let God lead them through their struggles and help them find the happiness they desired. I'm hoping if you're facing struggles now that you'll let God see you through. And I'm hoping that, like Troy and Destiny, you will let God be a part of your relationship, so that you also have that bond of three that isn't easily broken.

I enjoy mixing facts and fiction in my novels, and you'll learn about some of the truths hidden within the story on my website, www.reneeandrews.com. While you're there, you can also enter contests for cool prizes. If you have prayer requests, there's a place to let me know on my site. I'll lift your request up to the Lord in prayer. I love to hear from readers, so please write to me at renee@reneeandrews.com. Find me on Facebook at www.Facebook.com/AuthorRenee-Andrews. And follow me on Twitter at www.Twitter.com/ReneeAndrews.

Blessings in Christ,

Renee Andrews

Questions for Discussion

1. Destiny promised her subscribers and advertisers that she would run Troy's love letters, but she didn't have the authority to print them. Have you ever made a promise that was impossible to keep? How did you rectify the situation? What did you learn from it?

2. Troy started writing letters to his future bride as a preteen and then continued for fifteen years, defining what he wanted in a wife more clearly with each letter. Unfortunately, he set the bar so high almost no one fit the bill. Was he too picky, or did he have the right idea for finding a mate?

3. Troy's family was large and close-knit. Destiny's family was smaller and hadn't yet found that type of familial bond. How did their family backgrounds affect the way they perceived relationships as adults? How does your family background affect your relationships as an adult?

4. What do you think of Troy's reputation of dating someone once or twice, then not going out with her again if she wasn't what he deemed as marriage material? Do you think he approached this correctly, or should he have given himself more time to get to know each lady?

5. What qualities should a person look for in a spouse? Did you look for these qualities when

you dated, or if you are dating now, are you look-ing for those qualities?

6. Destiny wanted to be a published author, but she had a fear of submitting her work. Have you ever let fear keep you from obtaining a goal? What can a person do to overcome that fear?

7. Troy described the bond he wanted to have with his wife as the type of bond described in Ecclesi-astes 4:12, where a cord of three isn't easily bro-ken. Do you believe, as Rita suggested, that the difference in a marriage making it or not depends on whether God is included in the equation?

8. Destiny described the different feel of the small-town church in Claremont and her larger church in Atlanta. Have you visited small-town and big-city churches? If so, did you detect a difference, too?

9. Destiny's mother started out as a primarily mis-erable person, in spite of everything she had ma-terially. Why do you believe she wasn't happy?

10. Troy's family was obviously a big part of his life. Do you think it's advantageous to a marriage to have a family nearby when a couple is starting out? Or do you see it as a hindrance?

THE BOSS'S BRIDE
The Heart of Main Street
Brenda Minton
Gracie Wilson ran from her wedding and the man who broke her heart...straight into the arms of the man who might change her life.

A FATHER'S PROMISE
Hearts of Hartley Creek
Carolyne Aarsen
When the child she gave up for adoption shows up in town with her adoptive father, Renee must overcome her past to find true love.

NORTH COUNTRY HERO
Northern Lights
Lois Richer
It takes the tender heart of Sara Kane and her teen program to make a wounded former soldier see that home is where he belongs.

FALLING FOR THE LAWMAN
Kirkwood Lake
Ruth Logan Herne
Opposites attract when a beautiful dairy farmer who's vowed never to date a cop falls for the handsome state trooper who lives next door.

A CANYON SPRINGS COURTSHIP
Glynna Kaye
When a journalist arrives in town, will her former sweetheart resist her charms or find a second chance for love?

THE DOCTOR'S FAMILY REUNION
Mindy Obenhaus
After ten years away, Dr. Trent Lockridge hadn't counted on running into Blakely, the girl he should have married. Or the shock of finding out he has a son.

Look for these and other Love Inspired books wherever books are sold, including most bookstores, supermarkets, discount stores and drugstores.

REQUEST YOUR FREE BOOKS!

2 FREE INSPIRATIONAL NOVELS
PLUS 2
FREE
MYSTERY GIFTS

Love Inspired

LI13R

SPECIAL EXCERPT FROM

Love Inspired

*Gracie Wilson is about to become the most famous
runaway bride in Bygones, Kansas. Can she find true
happiness? Read on for a preview of
THE BOSS'S BRIDE by Brenda Minton.
Available September 2013.*

Gracie Wilson stood in the center of a Sunday school classroom at the Bygones Community Church. Her friend Janie Lawson adjusted Gracie's veil and again wiped at tears.

"You look beautiful."

"Do I?" Gracie glanced in the full-length mirror that hung on the door of the supply cabinet and suppressed a shudder. The dress was hideous and she hadn't picked it.

"You look beautiful. And you look miserable. It's your wedding day—you should be smiling."

Gracie smiled but she knew it was a poor attempt at best.

"Gracie, what's wrong?"

"Nothing. I'm good." She leaned her cheek against Janie's hand on her shoulder. "Other than the fact that you've moved one hundred miles away and I never get to see you."

What else could she say? Everyone in Bygones, Kansas, thought she'd landed the catch of the century. Trent Morgan was handsome, charming and came from money. She should be thrilled to be marrying him. Six months ago she had been thrilled. But then she'd started to notice little signs. She should have put the wedding on hold the moment she noticed those signs. And when she knew for certain, she should have put a stop to the entire thing. But she hadn't.

"Do you care if I have a few minutes alone?"

"Of course not." Janie gave her another hug. "But not too long. Your dad is outside and when I came in to check on you the seats were filling up out there."

"I just need a minute to catch my breath."

Janie smiled back at her and then the door to the classroom closed. And for the first time in days, Gracie was alone. She looked around the room with the bright yellow walls and posters from Sunday school curriculum. She stopped at the poster of David and Goliath. Her favorite. She'd love to have that kind of faith, the kind that knocked down giants.

"You almost ready, Gracie?" her dad called through the door.

"Almost."

She opened the window, just to let in fresh air. She leaned out, breathing the hint of autumn, enjoying the breeze on her face. She looked across the grassy lawn and saw…

FREEDOM.

To see if Gracie finds her happily-ever-after, pick up
THE BOSS'S BRIDE
wherever Love Inspired books are sold.

A FATHER'S PROMISE
by
CAROLYNE AARSEN

When the child she gave up for adoption shows up in
town with her adoptive father, Renee must overcome
her guilt to find true love.

*Available September 2013
wherever Love Inspired books are sold.*

www.LoveInspiredBooks.com

LI87836